By the Sword

A HWA SHORT STORY COLLECTION

Published in 2020 by Sharpe Books.

CONTENTS

A HWA SHORT STORY COLLECTION

The Plantagenet Princess by Paul Bannister

Well conscious of his status as a king's man, Justice Richard de Belers rode proudly at the forefront of his considerable entourage when he went to dine with the Earl of Leicester. He did not know that cold January day in the Year of Our Lord 1326 would be his last. He was not to feast with the earl: instead, he would sup with the Devil and he would not be using a long spoon.

On his final day alive, de Belers and his 45 servitors travelled alongside the winter-sere banks of the River Wreake on their way to Leicester Castle, but he never reached his destination and few mourned him, for he was a hated, venal judge, a baron of the Exchequer of Pleas who had cast his lot with the rogues who were looting England's treasury. He would not die for his high crimes, but for his arrogance and threats to his neighbours.

Much of this escaped me on that afternoon, for I was only a boy of 13 years. I had accompanied my father Sir Robert de Holland, Baron Holland of Lancashire and we were sitting our horses, concealed inside a copse of evergreens close to the road from Melton to Leicester. A dozen or so armed horsemen in helmets and breastplates sat with us, intently watching the roadway and gentling their steeds to quiet them. Father had told me our fellow watchers were members of the Folvilles, neighbours of the corrupt judge and victims of his thefts and threats.

"He won't be long now, Thomas," said Father. "It will be dusk in an hour or so and he's going to see Wryneck at Leicester Castle, so he still has seven or eight miles to travel." I shivered, and not with cold. "Wryneck, Father?" "Lord Henry of Lancaster is his real name, but he has a stiff neck and his head is turned." I nodded. Father was always patient with my questions. I whispered the next one, though. "Will they kill him?" Father looked at me then glanced away towards the other horsemen. "They will," he said curtly. "Or he would kill or incarcerate them. You'll see."

He paused and scratched his beard. "It's time you knew that evildoers can be brought to justice. Just do not tell your mother everything you see." I nodded. "I won't." I was well aware she would only worry, and possibly berate Father for taking me, but I was glad to be there, nervous, but excited, too.

"Shush, boy," he murmured. "They're coming."

Our whole group stirred and I glimpsed a double file of mounted men trotting towards us. A grandly-dressed man in a floppy velvet hat and scarlet cloak rode at the head of the column and this, I knew, was why we were here. Father had explained it. The man in the scarlet cloak was one of the five royal judges, a man of considerable power, but his influence went much, much further. He was a crony of the two Hugh Despensers, a father and son who were bleeding dry the treasury of King Edward II, the weak and malleable king who was the intimate friend of the younger Despenser, his chamberlain. With extortion, theft and false accusations, the duo swept up vast estates and wealth and de Belers, as their corrupt judicial agent, enforced judgements in their favour.

I heard a low growl from the men around me. Six or seven of them levelled war bows through the fir branches, the rest quietly eased swords and knives from scabbards There was a hissing noise as the arrows spun out of the greenery and then everyone but me was spurring forward.

I did as Father had commanded and stayed behind although I had to rein in my palfrey Garnet as she wanted to run with the other mounts. The shouting and yells of pain made Garnet ramp about and I had to pull hard on her bridle to steady her. By the time I could view the road again, ours were among Belers' men, slashing and striking, but it was not an even contest. The ambushers were soldiers but their victims were mostly servants, not fighting men and they turned and spurred away in panic. It was like a fox on chickens..

The man in the scarlet cloak was unhorsed and started to run, clumsy in his riding boots, towards a willow-lined brook to the north but a big, bearded man on a bay gelding clubbed him to the ground. "Take my land? Have me arrested? You foul scum!" he shouted and his sword fell two, three times against Belers' neck. The horseman leaned down to wipe his blade on the inert figure, nodded grimly and turned his horse's head away. The whole ambush was over in what seemed like a few dozen heartbeats.

Father left the group and rode to me. "That was the Folvilles at work, and efficiently, too, although it was a la Zouche who did the assassination." he said. "Master Belers will steal no more lands." I was shaken and guiltily exhilarated by what I had witnessed and my instinct told me that bad things would happen from it. And they did.

The murderous ambush caused King Edward to declare as outlaws the seven Folville brothers, Father and several La Zouches. Most fled to France; Father went to Wales but was caught and incarcerated at Warwick Castle. In time he escaped and, like the Folvilles and La Zouches, he joined Queen Isabella and the army she raised in France to overthrow the Despensers. She landed on the south coast of England with only 1,500 soldiers but Englishmen flocked to her and the army soon swelled.

Isabella regained the throne, pardoned her supporters, including the Folvilles, and cruelly executed the Despensers.

In turn Isabella's son seized the throne, exiled the queen and executed her lover. Followers of Thomas of Lancaster, brother of the lord whom de Belers had ridden to meet, added to the turmoil of blood. They caught my father and killed him for a long-ago act of refusing to support rebellion.

Now aged 19, I was a trained soldier and sought justice for my father's murder. The Folvilles had formed a force with other local families to combat the judiciary that was plundering England. "We are battling the Antichrist, Thomas," Eustace Folville told me. "We are supported by Sir Robert Tuchet, a lord of the Peak; we have even been given commissions by the religious, including the prior at Sempringham and the abbot at Haverholm. They want us to retrieve lands and goods stolen from them and from their parishioners."

The Folvilles were seen as honest and law-abiding protectors by the locals who knew them. The fourth son, Richard Folville was even ordained rector of the Church of the Holy Trinity at Teigh, near Melton. In a time when disputes were often resolved only by force, the brothers and their allies were acclaimed and aided by those oppressed by the judiciary.

With my father's murder, I had become the next Baron Holand and was myself a target for avaricious judges eager for my lands, so I chose to join the Folvilles. We kept the peace, caught those who extorted money from the citizenry

4

or who pretended to be royal tax collectors and pocketed the silver. We unmasked judges who took money from both sides in legal disputes or who relaxed penalties in return for bribes, but some called us outlaws, as did a corrupt royal judge, Richard de Willoughby of Nottingham.

He had seized land from the Coterel family, who fought his ruling, but hotheads from the Coterels and la Zouches responded to provocation and committed violence and we had word that Willoughby was coming to arrest us.

Eustace Folville, the leader of our group warned: "Willoughby is Chief Justice of the King's Bench while Edward is in France, but he does not act in the king's interests, only in his own, and is building great wealth and power. He has estates in 19 counties and manors in nine more, all acquired through corruption. He has built his wealth by seizing mining and fishing interests; he has a law career rooted in bribery and has made lucrative marriages that put him in the top ranks of England's most powerful knights.

"He has done this despite the nation being impoverished by plague, war and internal conflict. If he captures us, we will be hanged and illegally stripped of all our estates, for his own enrichment. We must stop him." And so we planned another ambush, like that in which we took Belers.

Willoughby came south from York on the Great North Way that runs through Sherwood and on to London. He must have thought his lofty rank alone would protect him, for he rode with just four men, enough to deter a highwayman, but not enough to scare Eustace Folville's brothers. One of them, Richard Folville was an expert archer and shot two of the judge's escort from their saddles before the others even knew what was happening.

The skirmish was over in moments, Willoughby and his two survivors were hooded and bound and we vanished into the great forest. The next several weeks were miserable ones for my lord Willoughby. He was kept chained to trees as we moved from camp to camp while his guards were sent off with a ransom demand. In time the money came, 1,300 marks to be handed over at a riverside alehouse in the hamlet of Farndon, near Newark. We cautiously viewed the rendezvous a few hours before the agreed time. As we expected, Willoughby's stewards brought soldiers, whom they hid in a barn near the alehouse.

Walter Folville arrived openly, collected the silver from two of the judge's servants, stepped outside and was into a waiting ferryboat and pulling hard across the broad River Trent before the hidden soldiers could gallop upstream and find a crossing.

Walter brought the silver to our forest hideout and two of the Folvilles and I were delegated to take it to my father's old comrade, Robert Moore, now a serjeant at the Common Bench at Westminster. He would safely hold the money as his connection through me to the Folvilles was not suspected. We handed over the silver and Robert suggested we walk out to view the Templars' old church nearby. There, alongside the river, I met Robert's cousin, the loveliest creature I then or ever since set my eyes upon.

Her name was Joan Plantagenet, she was a cousin of the king and she dazzled me. She wore a green gown with pearls, she was of medium height, with auburn-red hair, grey-green eyes and an unsullied complexion. Her teeth were white and straight, her lower lip hinted in its fullness at a loving passion yet to be awakened.

My eyes took in the slender neck that led gracefully to a pretty bosom, silver-belted little waist and a hint of curving thighs beneath her fine dress. I looked up again, and she giggled merrily. "Did your view give you pleasure, Master Thomas?" She said it with a murmur of laughter in her voice. I made my best leg and bowed low to hide the blush that was heating my face. Whatever I stammered made her laugh happily, and as we talked, the next hour flew faster than a stooping peregrine.

She left when a ladies' maid came to find her and I desperately whispered when might I see her again? "My cousin Robert may help," she said demurely, and I caught the least hint of white teeth at her lower lip as she made a secret smile. And she was gone. The Folville brothers teased me gently about me so obviously being smitten, but I made no mind. I was making my own private plans.

Back in Leicestershire, Richard de Willoughby was released as promised, but only after he swore a solemn oath of loyalty to the Folvilles. It was an oath he broke at once, pressuring a keeper of the King's Peace, Sir Robert Coalville to raise the hue and cry for the Folvilles. A *posse comitatus* was gathered. "They were too scared to come after us in the forest or at Ashby Folville," Eustace told us bitterly as we gathered at the fortified manor house in Ashby. "So they went after poor Richard at his church in Teigh."

Richard Folville was not just a man of religion, he was a skilled archer described as 'savage and audacious' by Willoughby, so the justice sent 20 men to capture him.

"The skirmish went on for two hours," Eustace told us. "My brother barricaded himself in the church and shot dead at least one of Coalville's men and we think he wounded several more. Eventually, Coalville lied, telling Richard he could leave in peace and speak his case before the king's justices. My brother had little choice: his arrows had run out, his two fellow defenders were wounded.

"He trusted Coalville," said Eustace, "but the treacherous vermin seized him and beheaded him in his own churchyard, without trial or absolution."

The death marked a change in the Folvilles and although the pope ordered Coalville and his troops to be whipped at each of the main churches in the region as penance for killing an ordained priest, the family sought revenge and became more violent. They indulged in looting, kidnapping, rustling and highway robbery, so I left them without regret and returned to Windsor and a more lawful life as a soldier.

Over the next few years as I campaigned in Flanders and France with Lord Edward of Woodstock, later to be called the Black Prince, I learned that King Edward had uncovered some of Willoughby's misdeeds. "He has been selling the laws of the land as if they were cattle or oxen!" raged the monarch, who demoted the judge and imprisoned him at Corfe Castle. When Willoughby confessed and threw himself on Edward's mercy, he was heavily fined, then sent to travel around the circuit courts of the nation to admit his misdeeds and answer local complaints about them.

But that was of little consequence to me. I had been irresistibly drawn to London, where with Robert Moore's help as a go-between, I was to secretly meet my Plantagenet princess Joan of Kent, at St Michael's church in Sittingbourne. This was a town busy with Canterbury pilgrims, where we could be anonymous.

Our romance was intense but hasty because I had taken

the Cross and must leave for Prussia on crusade. Joan told me she was 15 years of age, so was old enough to marry – the lower limit was 12 years – and we pledged to be handfast to each other in a private, legal marriage that was made without benefit of clergy or witnesses. We were young and hot-blooded, I was soon leaving the country again, so we consummated our love even though we did not have King Edward's permission to marry. After all, I reasoned, Edward was not even in England to grant his permission, and he would not be likely to deny his beautiful cousin anything, would he? After a few snatched and glorious days, I rode to Dover to join the crusaders.

In the time I was away, much happened. My absence stretched much longer than I expected, I fought in Prussia and Flanders, then raided right through France on campaign with the Black Prince. We made great *chevauchees,* moving fast with mounted archers and harassed King Philip's subjects with fire and sword. Once, we were almost trapped by the French but God's hand was upon us and our miraculous escape across the River Somme saved our weary troops to fight another day.

That great day came at the nearby village of Crecy where the Black Prince truly won his spurs and my archers shot the French nobility flat. We drove off the tired Genoese, King Philip's only professional soldiers, with a storm of arrows and we slaughtered 16,000 common soldiers and about 1,500 knights.

The battle was not without near-disaster. At one time, the prince was beaten to the ground, his standard bearer killed and banner captured, but the king sent reinforcements to rescue his unconscious son and my friend Sir Thomas

9

Danyers of Tabley, who was sheriff of Cheshire, hacked and slashed his way into the French ranks and retrieved the royal standard.

At day's end, every Englishman owned a fortune in loot or promised ransom money. I had enough gold to build several abbeys and fund the handful of farms each would require to sustain them for ever. I also had a priceless religious relic: a great shard of the True Cross, plundered by a Frenchman at the fall of Constantinople.

We triumphed at Crecy, but not all was sweetness and light. I found that my lovely Joan had been wedded to the Earl of Salisbury, a young knight who had influenced her mother Margaret to coerce the girl into marrying him. Later, Joan would explain that she dared not reveal our prior, secret marriage because we had not sought the king's permission and she feared for my safety if Edward discovered the union.

However, I chose to risk the king's wrath and sent what fortune was in my possession to the Pope with a petition to persuade him to annul Joan's marriage to Salisbury. I thought long and hard about what would sway His Holiness. Gold, to open the door, and the promise of a holy relic should convince him of my sincerity. Acquiring the shard of the Cross was heaven-sent, hopefully, I thought, that was its exact source.

I wrote a note to my Joan: "I have gained much treasure and a relic of the True Cross, which I may send to the Pope himself to ensure he rules for us in the matter of our marriage. This cannot be seen as a bribe but merely as the return of the holiest of relics to its rightful place."

There was no question of sending the sacred gift across war-torn France, where we were besieging Calais, so to secure the its safety, I sent it back to Joan in Kent with a wounded comrade. Then came rumblings of a Scots invasion of northern England, and Edward dispatched me to muster a force to turn them back.

In my absence, my Lord Salisbury, William Montacute learned of my petition to the Pope and poisoned the well for me. He told the king I planned to use Joan's Plantagenet name and my vast Crecy fortune - which Edward had not yet disbursed – to usurp the throne. "He is an adventurer, sire," he told the king. Edward, eager to gain the fortune he held for me, declared me traitor and issued my death warrant. On that very day came news that the Pope had accepted my fine, believed our sworn statements about our secret wedding and would annul Joan's marriage to Salisbury on receipt of the Cross relic.

I did not dare to return to Calais to argue my case with the king, but I wrote to the Black Prince, my old comrade in arms, and appealed to his chivalry. "Your cousin herself will testify on pain of her immortal soul that we are truly married. This she will swear on any sacred relic – and I have a piece of the True Cross which she holds safe. Her union with Salisbury is the result of her mother seeing an advantageous marriage to a nobleman and forcing a young girl into it. Lord Edward, you cannot in chivalry condemn your own blood to a cruel and sinful marriage."

Edward's response came to me in London and gave me joyful hope. "My father the king has heard from His Holiness and agrees to allow you to marry his cousin, or at least to let stand your present marriage, as attested to by our Holy Father.

"However, because of the insult you paid to the king by

11

marrying a Plantagenet without royal permission, you will forfeit the prizes you took on his campaign, which will include all the gold and silver, plate and vestments you took. You must also forfeit to him the most sacred relic of the piece of the One True Cross. If you fail to do these things, the death warrant remains viable."

My whole body sang with joy. I might be losing my fortune but I could create another, and Joan and I could be husband and wife. I saddled my horse and raced to her father's house in Kent, where her mother greeted me sourly, but I remained polite. "I am here to see my wife. The Pope has annulled her marriage to Salisbury," I said briefly. Lady Margaret looked stunned but resigned. Perhaps she had heard of the huge fortune I had won, which was in fact no longer mine, but I was not about to make that too clear.

Joan flew into the room and embraced me. "The king agrees," I said. "The Pope annuls Montacute's foul act and the king agrees! My death warrant will be lifted." She heaved a great sigh of relief. "Now, my love," she said, "we can be properly together."

"I have more news," I said gently. "The king is keeping almost all of my fortune. I shall have to win more." She looked downcast, then brightened. "Can we afford our own home?" "Yes, of course," I said. "I have a hall and a little money in Lancashire. There is one more thing: I shall have to surrender the piece of the True Cross. It is a condition of having the warrant lifted."

"Oh, my love," said Joan happily, "you need not worry about that. I gave that holiest relic to my uncle, Bishop Ralph. He sailed for Rome a fortnight ago, to give it to the Pope himself, in gratitude for the annulment."

I slumped onto the nearest stool. I had no fortune, no relic, no permission to marry and a royal death warrant on my head. *Deus Vult.*

The 'Plantagenet Princess' story is set between Thomas de Holland's campaigns with the Black Prince told in 'Storm of Arrows' which ended at Crecy and the sequel (working title 'Havoc' 2020) which will take Thomas up to Poitiers.

Author biography:

Englishman Paul Bannister spent his journalism career on national newspapers and the BBC in Britain and the USA and now makes his home in Oregon. He has two series published by Sharpe Books: the six 'Lost Emperor' volumes which begin with 'Arthur Britannicus,' and the 'Crusader' series of six, plus 'Storm of Arrows'(2019) and 'Murdering Nero.'(2020) All are available on Amazon, as is his autobiographical 'Tabloid Man & the Baffling Chair of Death.'

Interview with Paul Bannister

Can you tell us a bit about yourself? How long have you been writing and what other jobs have you had?

I joined a local weekly paper in Lancashire as a teen and worked on regional and national newspapers (Sun, Daily Mail, Telegraph) with a stint at the BBC before going to Florida and the National Enquirer. They sent me around the world a few times on assignments like unearthing the CIA's use of psychic spies. It's all in 'Tabloid Man and the Baffling Chair of Death' (Amazon), even the tale of sharing a sardine with Prince Charles and (not at the same time) being groomed by a gorilla versed in sign language.

What inspired you to write this particular story?

My 2019 book 'Storm of Arrows' has the real Sir Thomas Holland as its main character and his story is continued in my next book which takes the narrative from Crecy to the Battle of Poitiers. This period is the backdrop to a tale of the Folville clan of Leicestershire. They resisted the oppressive officials who were looting estates both royal and private. Thomas Holland is present as a young boy when the Folvilles ambush Edward II's corrupt baron of the Exchequer, an enabler for the throne-plundering Despensers.

If you were transported back to the time your story is set, who is the first person you would want to talk to, and

why?

If someone stumbles across a TARDIS, I'd love to use it to meet Thomas Holland. He rose from relatively humble beginnings to be elected to the Order of the Garter and was also a member of Henry III's Round Table; he married the great beauty of the age: Joan of Kent, a Plantagenet princess (their marriage was controversial and features in the story) and he campaigned with the Black Prince across France.

If there was one event in the period that you could safely witness, what would it be?

I'd like to observe the battle of Crecy, an important hinge of history. It may be my lifetime of playing rugby which inspires the wish, but I'd like to have seen the conflict which established the longbow as the deadliest weapon of its century and built a foundation for England's new importance in Europe.

Why do you think readers are still so thirsty for stories from this period?

England's growth of power and influence began here and is comprehensible: an army with hand weapons fighting at close range in relatively small numbers is more easily understood than is cyber warfare or destruction by missiles fired from thousands of miles away. Our ancestors succeeded in creating one of the world's greatest nations, we're rightly proud of them.

What are you writing at the moment?

After writing a Roman murder mystery, it's back to straightforward historical fiction as Holland campaigns again with the Black Prince. I'm more comfortable with the familiar – I have two suites of six books each, one set in Roman Britain, the other set around the Crusades. My interest is personal: my ancestor Robert Banastre fought for Duke William at Hastings and the Bannisters held Bank Hall, Bretherton since the 11th Century. The Norman hall was rebuilt in the 17th century but records in Preston show that Thurstan Banastre was born there in 1116, a Lancashireman like myself.

Where can readers find out more about your books?

As a measure of my own technological ignorance, I confess that my own website baffles me. **(bannisterbooks.com)** I once could make changes to it, now I'm unable to update it so my latest books, including the 2020 'Murdering Nero,' my first crime histfict, aren't even on there. At least, Amazon has them all.

Childish Things by Hana Cole

The boy reaches down to the bow scabbard and plucks an arrow from its quiver. Anticipation fizzing in his chest, he wheels his mare round, and gripping tight with his legs, steadies himself for the shot. He exhales. The world stills. His forefingers slacken, and the arrow goes eddying towards the target. The instant he releases the shot he knows it will be a bull's eye: from 150 feet, at a canter. Just like a real Mohammedan. Gui lifts his arms in triumph.

'For Jerusalem!' His elder brother raises his practise sword, and canters towards him. Throwing himself from his horse, Simon takes a running leap, and catching Gui by the legs, wrestles him from his mount. He hits the earth flat on his back with such force it feels as though his lungs have exploded.

'Convert and I will spare you,' yells his brother, leaning his weight onto Gui. At fifteen, Simon is three years older, broader and stronger too, but he does not share Gui's ability as a horseman, nor has he the eye of an archer. For all the punches he rains down on his younger brother, they are glancing blows against the truth. He will never have Gui's natural skill and he knows it.

'Renounce your sin and follow the true God!'

'Never!'

Younger, smaller – the second son – Gui he knows he cannot win this game of crusaders. Still, it is all the thrill in the world to play, even the unenviable part of the vanquished Saracen, and pinned underneath his older brother, he is laughing so hard he thinks his ribs might break. Breastbone still burning from the tumble, he thrashes to be free of the weight, but Simon holds firm until Gui begins to wheeze; choking and laughing at the same time.

Simon leans in harder, the victor's glint in his eye. His pride restored, he is laughing too now. The moment before the pressure becomes more than Gui can bear, Simon releases him, and they collapse into an exhausted embrace - the battle a fair draw.

A shadow cuts out the light above them: their father has arrived to supervise Simon's training.

'Gui, your tutor is here,' his father says.

'Please, father. Just a few minutes more?' It takes Gui all the courage he has to ask.

The big man's voice lifts. 'I do not require you to learn arms. I require you to study. And I require you to obey. When will you learn your place, boy?'

Gui hangs his head. The game is over.

***

'Well, Master Gui?'

The tutor's voice jolts Gui from his reverie. His eyes sweep down to the text. He stares at it for a few moments, but as well as he knows it, he cannot answer a question he has not heard.

'Should I read?' he hazards.

His tutor smiles benignly. Gui reckons him to be around thirty. Straggly hair retreats from his wide temple, and despite his badly-nourished frame, he carries a small, perfectly round paunch from all the hours he spends bent over in study. Gilles is a former student at Chartres cathedral and Gui likes him well enough. He is both lenient and patient, resigned to all the things he once hoped to achieve but has not.

'Who has the greater virtue, Master Gui. The slave or the master?'

Gui lifts his chest. He knows this.

'Augustine believed that slavery did more harm to the slave owner than the enslaved person. The humble station does as much good to the servant as the proud position is detrimental to the master.'

'Good.' Gilles flicks distractedly through the text. He has never bothered to conceal his preference for the trouvères' courtly rhymes.

Although the window is shuttered, it does not stop the enticing sounds of spring from filtering in; the shrill of birdsong, the groundsmen clearing away the last of winter's brush, the lewd gossip of housemaids that is supposed to be beneath Gui's station and his sex. Worst of all, is the sound of his brother still training at arms in the yard.

Outside Simon's whoop carries across the courtyard. Instinctively Gui turns; has he hit the quintain, sent it spinning without being unseated by the twirling arms? He slumps. The day is heating up and the sun's rays angle through the wooden slates, warming his back.

His tutor glances towards the light source. 'You may open them,' he says, rummaging in his bag. 'We will break before geometry.'

Geometry: the signature of the Master Craftsman. Will he ever unpick the God's secrets if he cannot pay attention to the foundations? Are they even meant for him anyway? Gui throws open the shutters. If he jumps up and leans out over the sill, he can just about see his big brother practising his knightly skills.

Gui closes his eyes, inhales the sunshine, reliving that morning's freedom, those brief moments when he had shown his excellence. And been more than a second son destined for the Church. Tomorrow morning he will not let Simon drag him from his horse so easily. His tutor rings the small bell on his table. Gui delays for a moment, letting the warmth flood over him.

'Sire! Sire!' The voice of his father's marshal carries through the air, as unmistakeable as the urgency of his tone.

He and Gilles exchange glances as his father passes by the window, barking at his men. More voices join the hubbub; something is going on. His tutor chews his lip as though he is considering some profound point of philosophy - which Gui knows means he is weighing up an opportunity to get back to his beloved trouvères. He probably wanted to be one, thinks Gui, and the idea of this gangly, awkward man wooing a lady of the court makes him snigger into his sleeve. Inwardly he urges his tutor to dismiss him so he can go and see what the raucous is all about, but, almost as though he can sense Gui's desire, Gilles says, 'A bit more grammar, then you can go.'

As fast as Gui races through the fourth and fifth declensions, by the time he gets outside, not so much as a speck of dust remains of the excitement. He chases round to the stables where he manages to extract from one of the stable hands that the Lord of Thymerais's men have encroached on his father's land out by the Perche forest again. The count gave the territory to his father for service several years before, but it's good grain land and there have been skirmishes about the rights more than once. His father has departed with two dozen men and sent word for more, the stable boy tells him. Simon has gone with them.

Gui presses his lips together. Simon. He huffs at the unfairness of it. The voice in his head reminds him that his father didn't let Simon ride to battle when he was twelve either. But Simon was nowhere near as skilled as he is. Nowhere near. Besides, bishops field armies too, he mumbles sullenly. Why shouldn't he join them? Most of the sons of noble houses have their first taste of a fight around his age. It feels humiliating to be left behind– like the time his mother made him go to bed in the summer when it was still light and Simon and all his friends were still playing outside. How they had mocked him, 'baby's going to his crib.' He flushes crossly at the memory.

Anyway, he tells himself as he stomps over to his mare, Candice, perhaps they could use my help. In a year's time he will be sent away to the Cathedral school at Chartres. It is an honour really, a place where you can make something of yourself, even if you haven't had the luck to be born in the right order. But it feels like an exile to Gui, and he knows whatever happens after, however well he equips himself, he won't get this time back. A gap will develop between him and his brother that will never be bridged. And his father will be even less interested in him than he is now - if that is even possible. He and Simon make a good team. He can mount a horse with Simon, riding at a canter. Easy. Under the right circumstances they could really achieve something to talk about. He imagines his father's face witnessing their deeds of great valour – he'll have no choice but to be proud. He has no idea what Gui is capable of.

Before he knows it, he has tacked up Candice, and is

21

hunting around for his weapons. *What are you doing?!* The voice is so urgent he half thinks there is another person in the stables, and it is not just him, trying to talk himself out of something that he knows he absolutely shouldn't be doing. There is a throbbing sensation in the pit of his stomach as he realises he is actually going to do it.

Without waiting for the demons of doubt to do further damage, he grabs his bow and sword – which is in fact just one of his father's old arming swords. Then, a quick check round to make sure there are no witnesses and he is off, heart skipping as he canters along the lane, churning up great whirls of dust.

With his father's retinue least a mile or two ahead, Gui tears up the gorse-covered plains as fast as he dare. They will be there by now, exchanging hot words with Thymerais's men. Both men have come for a fight, so the verbal exchange will not last long. The thought that it will be all over by the time he gets there makes him feel as though he has ants crawling all over him. In his haste to leave, he has forgotten to bring water with him, and as he nears the outskirts of the commune, his mouth is bone dry with anticipation. *You stupid boy, how you could you forget such a simple thing?* When he scolds himself it is always his father's voice he uses.

He trains his eyes and ears on his surroundings. The river, concealed by long-eared rushes, is a league or so away to his right, another smaller tributary runs a few hundred yards ahead – he can stop and drink there, then approach the hamlet, keeping to the edge of the forest. This is where his mare comes into her own: small, light footed and a boring mid brown colour – how disappointed had he been when he discovered she wasn't bay or chestnut – but she will be tricky to spot against the backdrop of the wheat fields and woodland.

Gui is so busy thinking through all the things he knows are important, that he almost doesn't hear the voices; men whispering on the other side of the gorse. If his memory serves him right, there is a small hillock just beyond - the highest point in this land of endless wheat fields. They must be a couple of his father's scouts, sent up there on their bellies and now returning. Must be.

Gui slips down from Candice and inches forward in a crouch. The voices are coming his way. He squats and waits. It's probably his father's squires, he tells himself again as his hands start to dampen. The voices fall silent, although he can still hear their footfall. It isn't swishy though, like it would be if they were dragging their feet through the grass, more of a soft pad and rustle, which tells Gui they are picking up their feet and placing them down carefully. Do they know he is there?

'To the left,' comes the whisper.

Gui holds his breath as two pairs of legs emerge, feet from his face. He rocks back silently onto his heels and reverses himself into the cover of the brush. Looking upward, his body melts with relief. 'Oh thank heaven, Roland,' he says, standing to greet his father's retainers. 'I thought it was…'

'Christ's bones it's Gui. Look out!' Roland cries, his face crumpling as Gui swings round to see two horsemen cantering towards them: Thymerais' men.

'Run!'

Gui throws himself onto Candice and hares across the stretch of open heathland, heart pumping acid through his veins. He makes for the cover of the forest, weaving through the silver birches and the pines, grunting like a boar fleeing a hunter's lance. Roland glides in at his flank.

'What in the devil's name are you doing here?' he yells, although Gui knows he doesn't want an answer. 'The skirmish has started up near the village. Your father sent us out to make sure there weren't more coming in from the other side of the river.'

Gui can't think. His horse is moving so quickly, it's all he can do to stop himself from being unseated by stray branches, or tumbling over the thick network of roots that carve steps and trips into the forest floor. Once it's clear they aren't being chased, they slow to approach the treeline once more.

'Jocelyn will try to draw them wide, back down towards the river,' says Roland. Immediately, the fist of dread bunches in Gui's stomach: if something happens to Jocelyn it will be his stupid fault. Why didn't he think of this? His father sent two scouts out to secure their position, and he has stumbled them right into an ambush. He pulls his hands down his face. How can he put this right?

'Your father's main contingent is over on the eastern side of the village. We should have more men arriving soon.'

'How many has Thymerais got?'

'About forty.'

'So he means to settle it once and for all.'

'Seems so.'

'We must warn father,' he says resolutely. 'Give him a chance to divert some men south. They'll be coming whether I'm here or not.'

Roland leans into his pommel, eyeing Gui reluctantly; the cost of warning his lord of an ambush against delivering the body of his son.

'Come on,' Gui pleads. 'You know what a good shot I am. We have to warn him now.'

'Stay by me,' says Roland.

They emerge from the forest, cautious as deer. The village is length of a couple of longbow shots ahead. A large water wheel straddles the stream that rings the southern edge. Just beyond it, the wooden pikes of a makeshift rampart jut up like broken teeth on the nearside of the main bridge. A melee of men parry back and forth across the ground: lances, swords, axes, mounted knights and infantry scythe at each other, raking up the earth and the dust. A skirmish Roland said, but it looks fierce to Gui.

'We'll go out wide. ' Roland points to where the treeline fingers out from the main forest in a tangle of shrubs, meeting with a dry stone wall that marks village grazing land. It's not dense enough to conceal them, but it gives them some cover as they advance.

 Gui trots forward. Suddenly, he doesn't feel quite so brave anymore. His grip on the reins feels slack, like he can't tighten his fingers properly. Roland scrutinises him and Gui feels the shame creep up his neck.

'I'm ready,' he says determinedly.

Roland cocks his head to one side. Gui gives a single, defiant nod. He absolutely cannot back out at this first shock. Not when his brother is among those hacking at each other just yards away.

They reach the stone wall when raised voices come skimming over the fields. Jocelyn is tearing across the plain, three mounted men in pursuit.

'Go!' Roland yells. 'Head for your father's line.'

Gui kicks into his mount's belly and they race towards the huddle of men in his father's livery. Sweat drips from his brow into his eyes. Instinctively, he inches his hand down to his bow scabbard and tugs his bow free. He only has five or six arrows with him, but they are bound tight in the quiver and he is going too fast to jerk them loose. His stomach feels as though it is being cinched by an ever-tightening belt. His hand and feet are lead.

One of the knights has peeled away from Jocelyn and is charging towards him. Never in all the battle games he and Simon have played has he faced a lance. His guts heat as he realises he is going to have to choose: either he digs in, aims for his father's line, and prays they don't get to him first, or he can slow down to take the shot, knowing he is going to be out-run if he misses. And he is going to have to choose now.

He pulls on the reins and Candice slows. An arrow slaps the ground just in front of them, then rebounds, skimming his horse. She rears up. Gui clamps his legs as hard as he can to bring her down. He tugs an arrow from the quiver as Roland thunders passed him, mace raised, towards the approaching knight.

Gui has twenty yards now. He loads his bow, closes one eye and lets his fingers release. It is such a well-practised gesture, as natural as his breath; an anchor in a world that is moving too fast. Gui silently exalts as the knight clutches his arm and attempts to retreat. But Roland doesn't pass up the opportunity, and brings his weapon down to meet the knight full in the face. All Gui sees is a spray of red as the man slumps on his mount. Gui's heart is hammering with shock as Roland doubles back to join him. The air splits open as a volley of arrows arc overhead. His father's squire is just paces away when he lurches forward, face contorted. Gui can only watch as Roland's horse tears off towards the trees, an arrow plainly visible in its rider's back. There is an awful hot, liquid sensation in his bowel that he prays does not mean he is going to be sick. Or worse.

A second knight races in. The voice in Gui's head is telling him to discard his bow and unsheathe his father's arming sword, but his hands are slippery, and his grip weak. He will feel more vulnerable with it. Roland's face dances in his mind's eye. The rider is upon him now and he can see he is not much older than his own brother. He cries out to give himself courage. Kicking his rouncey, he pushes his upper body forward, urging the mare to gain speed.

The other boy is up in his stirrups, sword raised. Gui tacks wide of the blow, gallops on to find some space. He turns, draws, fires blindly. He is aiming for the boy's shoulder but he glances the horse in the haunches. It screams, bucks. Still, the knight-boy raises his sword. Snorting now, breathless, Gui can feel the world spinning. He manages to duck his assailant's blade a second time but, as the knight swings his arm round, he finds the side of Gui's head with the pommel of his weapon. Then, Gui's head is ringing. He can hear blood pounding through his temples as he slips from his horse.

'Gui!'

He heaves himself to his feet, smears at the sweat and blood in his eyes. But he doesn't need clear vision to know it is Simon racing across the open ground towards him. The air crackles once more: Thymerais's archers have seen him.

'No!' he urges, but Simon is already committed.

'Give me your hand!'

Gui tries to lift his arm but his mind won't connect to his body. Paralysed, he can feel the warmth of his own blood trickling down his collar, the edges of the world darkening. The din of voices make one indistinguishable from the other. The sound of hooves thrum in his belly; someone is approaching from behind. Simon's arm waves down at him, insistent. Gui staggers forward, manages to hurl up his hand.

'Jump!' Simon screams. His brother's face is all he can see. His heart bursting against his ribs, he finds the force to swing himself upwards. Simon does the rest. Somehow he clings on, buffeted by the bump and jar of the horse as it pounds across the earth, its breath hunting. They are fifty yards from the ramparts now. Then, there is a hollow thud, and Simon collapses onto him, pierced. The horse rears up, unseating them both.

'No!' His cry does not sound human as he crawls to where his brother lies, moaning. It is a desperate howl: the sound of someone bargaining with God to undo a horror that cannot be undone. A tunnel of black is closing on him, tighter and tighter. Fringed blood red, the yellow glare of the sun penetrates the dark of his closed eyes. Then, there is nothing.

**

It's cool inside. Cool and gloomy. He isn't supposed to be here but he cannot bear to be anywhere else and the doctor does not have the heart to tell him to leave his sentry post outside Simon's chamber. He has no recollection of what happened after the fall, of how he got from the battlefield back home. From the look in his father's eyes, black and merciless as the devil himself, Gui knew better than to inquire. He didn't even dare to ask if his father had triumphed, or if the loss of his son had fractured their purpose.

All he knows is the stiff back of the walnut chair on which he sits, and the pale blue of the river in the tapestry that decorates the wall before him - a sip of reviving water he cannot take. And prayer. The supplication he should have been engaged in all along. If only. This is what happens when you question God's order. *When will you learn your place, boy?*

The doctor emerges, a tray of instruments and gore in his hand. Gui's shattered heart hammers as he tried to decipher the man's expression.

'He's alive. Just.'

Gui eyes cloud. He makes the sign of the cross. Thank you. Thank God.

'But he won't hold a sword again.'

Gui's chest heaves in and out as he fights to supress the sob that he has no right to cry.

At the edge of his vision, a long, thin shadow stretches along the corridor. He sniffs, braces himself – he has been waiting for this summons. No matter how violent his father's fury, there is no punishment that will equal this shame. Or the regret that squirms in the pit of his stomach like a bed of eels eating each other alive.

Gui stands, ready to follow the messenger to the physical assault he knows awaits. But all the butler says, is, 'You are to leave for the monastery at Chartres tomorrow at dawn.' Then he lowers his eyes, and turns on his heels, shuffling away until he merges with the dark, empty corridor.

Interview with Hana Cole

Can you tell us a bit about yourself? How long have you been writing and what other jobs have you had?

I've loved writing ever since I was a small child, but I didn't attempt a novel until I entered the world of 9-5 work!

I studied medieval history at university and loved it, but it seemed to me that some of the most important and interesting ideas were best developed in fiction. Not to mention the pull of good storytelling - as soon as my exams were over you would find me in the park with a Sharon Penman novel.

In terms of other jobs there have been quite a few. I've been a film subtitle translator, a yoga teacher and a financial analyst – so quite a mixed bag. I found it hard to settle as nothing compares to writing fiction.

What is it about the Medieval Period that inspires you?

I fell in love with the Medieval period when I first encountered it at school. It's such a rich tapestry. There is so much for the imagination to take hold of. From the visuals of frescoes, tapestries and romantic dresses, to the threads of dynastic political intrigue that run on for centuries.

I am also drawn to the spiritual depth and diversity of the period, which lead to such dramatic extremes - from sublime Gregorian chants, and the mysteries of the Abrahamic cosmologies, to the dreaded Inquisition.

What inspired you to write this particular story?

I think people associate the crusades with knights and Jerusalem, and the first three crusades are the ones that get most attention. The whole crusading era spanned several centuries though, and they were very much entwined with popular movements. I remember the Children's Crusade struck me as a particular horror when I was studying the period at university, and its story isn't widely known, so I was drawn to the idea of putting it out there.

The novel charts quite an epic journey – from Northern France to the Languedoc, then across the Med to Egypt and back. It gave me the opportunity not only to touch on other lesser-known crusades, such as the Albigensian Crusade against the Cathars in Provence, but also to delve a little into the fascinating world of Mamluk Egypt.

What do you enjoy most about writing?

Living with the characters. They kind of become like friends – sometimes it can feel as if you have opened up a corridor in time and are channelling a voice from the past that wants to be heard.

I very much enjoy bringing the past to life. The French historian Jules Michelet talked about history as resurrection, and the job of the historian as 'heating cooled ashes'. I feel as though the sources always hint at something more profound and interesting than the facts they reveal – and it's that speculation I find so compelling.

If you were transported back to the time your story is set, who is the first person you would want to talk to and why?

Well I'd certainly want to talk to someone who knew Stephen of Cloyes, the shepherd boy preacher of the Children's Crusade. I'd be interested to try and discover whether there was anyone coordinating what appeared to be a grass roots movement. I'd also be interested to speak to some of the merchants who worked out of Marseilles to see what truth there was to the rumours that some of the children were in fact sold into slavery from the port.

If there was one event in the period you could witness (in perfect safety) what would it be?

It's very hard to pick just one. Big battles such as the Battle of Hittin or the fall of Constantinople have a certain appeal as spectacles, but I think we filter them too much through film in our minds. In reality it would be too horrific to witness, so I'd go for something like watching Ambrogio Lorenzetti paint the frescoes of Good and Bad Government in Siena, or watching Charlemagne being crowned Holy Roman Emperor.

Why do you think readers are still so thirsty for stories from this period?

For much to same reason it appeals to me I guess. It is, I think, very much a time that allows people to believe in magic. It's sufficiently distant to really allow you to escape into it, and it is easy to romanticise the period. That said, there is probably also a bit of, "I'm glad I wasn't living then" rubber-necking that people enjoy – such as imagining life when your Doctor used leeches, or before modern dental surgery.

What are you writing at the moment?

I'm working on the first part of a thriller series set around the rise and fall of the first great merchant banking houses in the mid fourteenth century.

How important is it for you to be part of a community of writers, and why?

It can be difficult for writers sometimes, as it's an inherently solitary activity and I think a lot of writers are introverts by nature. That said, I do enjoy going to conferences and events and getting the chance to meet people – I've made friends through associations like the RNA and the HWA, as well as benefitting from the huge wealth of knowledge of other writers.

Where can readers find out more about your books?

Well this is my debut novel, and you can find it on Amazon, or you can find me on twitter @hanascribe

A Beggar's Coat by Jemahl Evans.

A large crowd was gathered on the Smooth Field for the Friday horse market. Set outside London's ancient walls and enclosed by the Fleet River to the west, the rough ground was used for fairs and trading by the citizens. The horse market was the most popular day for the royal court. There was more entertainment on show. The thick fall of overnight snow had been turned to muddy slush as races and gambling took place; jousts and scores settled, boots and hooves, all cut up the ground like a ploughed field. The combat was accompanied by the yells and whooping of the watching crowd, apprentices and shop boys mostly, who supped ale by the gallon and cheered their favoured contestants on, always causing more brawling and rowdiness among the rough crowd. The new priory hospital, Rahere's folly, at the south end of the field and close to the city walls would tend to the broken crowns. The monks would spend their weekend setting bones and restoring men struck senseless ready for the following Friday's display.

King Henry and his new Chancellor, Thomas of London, were sat atop riding horses, with guards and flunkeys in tow, taking the sights and sounds in. The contrast between the two men was stark: Henry, in his twenties, broad and flame haired, well muscled and barrel-chest, and in well made but unadorned leather armour and a broadsword at his side. His dark-haired slender Chancellor was perched on an expensive white horse, finely dressed with a fur trimmed cloak of red and grey stripes and fur hat to keep him warm in the biting wind.

'Who are these two?' Henry pointed to two men making ready to joust.

'The older man is Josselin of Pontivy, brother to the Count of Rohan.'

The King grunted. 'A Breton then.'

'He is renowned with the lance and has a fine seat,' said Thomas. 'And his brother could be important to us.'

There was a sniff at that comment from one of the nobles attending on the King. Thomas glanced behind at the barons. All of them were waiting for the common born Chancellor to slip and fall so they could take his favoured position. Thomas needed more noble allies. He turned back to the contest and pulled the fur trimmed cloak close.

Henry saw the glance. 'They will not divide us, my friend,' he whispered. Then he turned away and pointed to the field. 'And the other man, God's teeth, he is huge?' Henry pointed at a huge man riding a tall grey horse.

Thomas smiled at his excited lord. 'That is Reginald FitzUrse, Lord. He is a squire in your household. They call him the Bear because of his temper.'

'Ursus by name ursus by nature,' quipped Henry. 'How old is he?'

'Fourteen.'

The King whistled. 'Does his skill match his size?'

Thomas merely smiled and gestured for Henry to watch.

The Bear eyed the other warrior warily across the field. The boy had proved his mettle in practice bouts and with lads his own age, the other squires were terrified of FitzUrse, but Josselin of Pontivy was a veteran of nearly thirty years age.

Pontivy was good enough for it to be a prestigious bout for the Bear, but not so renowned that he would scorn the challenge from a petty squire. Both men wore heavy mail coats and mittens, open faced helms with a vertical bar running down the nose to protect the face from a slash, and flat topped kite shields on their left arm. Neither warrior wore surcoats in the cold weather, nor was Pontivy's shield was adorned by any design; it was but blank battered leather. FitzUrse pulled away the cloth covering on his own tall kite shield to reveal a crude image of a black bear painted on the face of the bleached white hide. One of the other squires had painted it on for him the night before. FitzUrse intended to make a name for himself that day.

'Give me a lance,' said Pontivy to his manservant.

The Breton was annoyed with the impudent lad who had challenged him. FitzUrse had baited the older warrior the night before, mocking his accent and his dress, calling him ancient.

'I am going to teach the whelp some manners.'

The servant handed him a long white ash lance tipped with an iron point. A deadly weapon in the right hands; these Friday bouts were no practice bout or tournament jostle. Men died if they were not careful or skilled enough to survive. Pontivy was starting to regret drinking so much ale the night before.

The Bear took a similar lance from an attendant and shook free his heavy wool cloak. Enclosed in a mail hauberk and leather gambeson, the bitter cold did not bother FitzUrse, but he did not want his cloak catching and causing disaster during the bout. He noted the Breton doing the same with his fur trimmed garment. The man was mounted on a brown stallion, which snorted steam and stamped its fore hooves as they waited. FitzUrse took up his position at the southern end of the field on his grey animal, perhaps sixty or so yards apart from the Breton. Once both men were ready, they saluted the King and his courtiers with their lances and kicked their horses up into a charge. There was no great ceremony, this was no tourney, but the crowd instantly started up with a great cheer at the battle.

The two armoured knights pounded towards each other on their horses, lances set, faces grim. FitzUrse aimed his weapon at the Breton's shield, as he had been trained, standing up in the stirrups at the point of impact and thrusting through as his lance shattered into a thousand splinters. The Breton had aimed at the Bear's head. FitzUrse felt it whistle along the side of his helmet but only glancing.

Bastard, thought the Bear. That could have killed me if he hit. FitzUrse threw away his broken lance and drew his father's sword, yanking on his horse's reins to wheel the beast about. The Breton had turned and was charging down at him again, the lance set ready to sewer the Bear. FitzUrse tucked his head down behind the flat top of his shield, barely peeping over it as the Breton closed. Pontivy's lance shattered on the Bear's shield. FitzUrse swayed back in his saddle at the force of the blow, and slashed at the Breton with his sword as Pontivy whistled past. Then he turned and stuck out at him again.

The Bear was angry, he had wanted to beat the man and earn a name for himself, but he had not intended to kill him. The Breton's strike at his face had enraged FitzUrse, insulted his standard of honour. He hammered his sword into the man's armoured back like he was at a forge before Pontivy could wheel to face him. The Breton felt the blow, he felt his ribs crack at the power of it, and his arm went numb as he desperately tried to pull his horse around, but he was too slow. He was trying to draw his sword, and the Bear struck him plum on the top of his helm and knocked him senseless. As the Breton slipped unconscious from his saddle, FitzUrse yelled in delight and turned to face the watching King and Chancellor.

Henry and Thomas both had wide grins on their faces.

'He is going to be a very good warrior, Lord King,' said Thomas. 'A champion in the tournaments.'

One of the barons behind them sneered. 'The boy was fortunate that is all. Had the Breton's lance been an inch to the right then he would have died on the first pass. What would a Cheapside clerk know of a warrior's skill?'

Thomas physically flinched at the noble's words. The King's barons were ever set on humiliating the low born Chancellor. Henry noticed his friend's discomfort.

'He knew enough to wager on the youngster,' said the King sharply. 'Whereas I see you lost betting on the Breton, Belleme.'

'Yes Lord,' the Baron looked suitably chastised but shot Thomas a vindictive glance as the King turned away.

Thomas saw the look but said nothing. He knew the nobles despised him as a common clerk not a warrior. He pulled his fine new grey and red cloak about him and turned back to the King.

'A new coat,' said the King.

'Yes,' said Thomas. 'It is most warming, and it looks good too.'

The King laughed at his Chancellor's vanity.

'I want some food,' said Henry, when he had composed himself. 'Back to Westminster to see what the kitchens have.' The King turned his horse and led it down the track that ran alongside the Fleet River with no further discussion.

Thomas turned his white mount to follow his King, and the other barons and knights of the royal household came on behind. Thomas could feel their glares; he could hear their whispered contempt.

'Do not let it bother you,' said Henry as the Chancellor pulled up alongside on the road.

'Lord?'

'These sycophants and weasels,' Henry gestured to the household. 'It is only my favour you need worry on and you ever have that, my friend. They will not divide us.'

'Still they will do what they can to undermine me in your eyes. They seek to remove me.'

Henry grunted at that. He knew the truth of Thomas's words. Outraged nobles had been complaining about the affront to their dignity in taking instruction from a lowborn London clerk ever since he made the man Chancellor. Archbishop Theobald had put Thomas in the King's service, but the clerk was efficient; he got things done; he was a loyal servant to his master. More than that, Henry liked him. Thomas made him laugh and had charmed his mother the Empress Matilda. The two of them together could remake Christendom. If only the barons could be brought into line. Henry noted a small bucktoothed beggar boy shivering on the cobbles by the gates as they arrived at Westminster palace. The lad was dressed in torn ragged clothes, whatever colour they had once been had faded to a dirty grey. No hat nor cloak, a smudged dirty face, he would freeze to death in the winter's night if he did not get some warmth. An idea suddenly occurred to the King.

'Do you see that lad?' asked Henry.

Thomas looked down at the ragged youth and smiled softly. 'I do, Lord?'

'How weak, and how poorly clad he looks!' said Henry. 'Don't you think it would be a great kindness to give him a thick and warm cloak?' He gave his Chancellor a sly grin.

'Certainly,' Thomas answered, laughing along with Henry. He understood his King's mind. 'You ought to have a mind and eye for such ills, oh generous and benevolent King.

They both pulled up their horses and looked down at the beggar boy, who cringed in fear at the great men and their snorting animals towering over him.

'Would you like to have a good cloak, Boy? To keep you warm?'

The lad looked terrified; keeping his eyes down and nodding. Was this some rich man's cruel jest to a beggar?

The King turned back to the Chancellor, 'Well then, you will give this great charity.'

Henry grabbed hold of Thomas's new and precious cloak of scarlet and grey that he had been flaunting all day, trying to rip it from the Chancellor's shoulders. Thomas was having none of the King's assault and pushed back at his monarch. Henry almost fell from his horse, swaying in his stirrups. The two of them scuffled on horseback, giggling all the while like a pair of naughty schoolboys, pulling the cloak back and forth between them. The beggar boy watched on, incredulous and aghast. This was a very sight, the King of England and his Chancellor at fisticuffs.

The rest of the royal household were arriving. The beggar tucked his head down and tried to keep away from the rowdy nobility. Henry's barons, knights, and soldiers looked dumbfounded at each other; all wondering what could have been the cause of such a sudden struggle, and not knowing what to do. Thomas and Henry paid them no heed as they scuffled, calling out bawdy taunts as they battled.

'I have a plan,' whispered Henry, as he grabbed Thomas by the head and knocked off his fur cap.

'Yes, Lord.'

Thomas finally gave way and allowed Henry to take the cloak from his shoulders and throw it to the beggar. The boy quickly wrapped himself in the coat – white faced and still worried – and gave thanks to God and the King for the gift.

'What is this?' asked one of the nobles.

Henry told them that it was the Chancellor's charity and a wondrous thing. Then he offered his own coat to Thomas. Henry had made his point to the Barons. Thomas and the King were as close as brothers. The slender Chancellor smiled at Henry's display, but turned down the King's offer of a cloak despite his shivers.

'We are here now, Lord,' he said, gesturing to the palace. 'There are warm fires and good wine inside.'

The barons could see that the two men were fast friends; any of them who planned to drive a wedge between the King and his Chancellor were dismayed. It seemed that nothing could divide them. Some of the Barons and courtiers flicked coins contemptuously at the beggar as they passed, others offered Thomas their cloaks. The Chancellor refused all offers of a coat from the nobles. He knew some would try to curry favour now. They would see him as their path to the

King. It was better than their hostility, he decided. He had a job to do and a lord to serve. Thomas would need the barons' support if he was to make Henry a great king.

FitzUrse the Bear arrived in the King's hall flushed with the success on Smooth Field. He had taken Pontivy's arms and horse from the victory. The animal he would keep but the arms could be traded. The young squire was not from a rich family, and his parents were both dead, but he hoped to gain an estate one day and the victory had set him on that path.

Henry saw the giant squire enter the hall. The King was sitting with Thomas at his side, on a small raised dais above the rowdiness. They had all been drinking since their return from the horse fair, and the King called the Bear to him.

'Yes, King.' FitzUrse bowed deeply.

'It seems you are a born warrior, young man,' said Henry. 'You have cost some of my barons' coin today with your win.'

FitzUrse did not know what to say to that. He did not wish to make enemies of the court.

'It is of no matter.' The Chancellor Thomas leaned forward with a wide grin on his face. 'The King and I both gained on *our* wagers.'

Henry burst out laughing and drained his cup of wine, taking another from a grey servant, and then fixed FitzUrse with a hard stare.

'You are still a squire?'

'Yes, King.'

Henry tugged at his belt, and undid his own sword. Made of fine Damascene steel and brought from Constantinople as a gift from the Roman Emperor on his coronation. It was worth a prince's ransom. He cast the weapon at the Bear, who deftly caught it with one hand.

'Keep it; I think you have earned your spurs.'

There were gasps of wonder from the audience at such a rich gift. The Bear fell to his knees to thank Henry, pledging to be his loyal warrior from that day forth. FitzUrse's eyes were shining with pride as the King raised him up.

'You shall be my loyal Bear.'

'I will follow you into Hell, Lord King,' the Bear said happily. 'Should you ever command.'

Thomas sat back and smiled quietly to himself. Everything was turning out exactly as he had hoped. He left Henry carousing with the Bear and his barons not long after, and walked down to his apartments by the Thames. As a boy he had played on these streets; he had run with the London crew. His parents were buried in the churchyard of St Pauls. He was a Londoner born and bred. Thomas could never escape that, he did not want to, but the great men of the kingdom held it against him.

The common born chancellor wished his mother was there to see his success. She would have been so proud; all her sacrifices to see her son educated were not in vain, Thomas thought to himself. I will be the best chancellor England has seen.

Thomas opened the door to his chamber. His new manservant was setting the fire in its hearth and trying to spark it into life. The bucktoothed young boy turned back to face his new lord, but now he was dressed in clean woollen breeches and tunic and his face was clean.

'You did well, Osbern of Dover,' said Thomas.

'The King did not recognise me, master?'

'Kings do not take much note of beggar boys' faces, or servants, or rabbits,' the Chancellor told Osbern cheerfully. 'But best to stay out of his way for a few days. There is no point in chancing fate.'

'Your plan worked then, Lord?'

'Yes,' said the Chancellor with a soft smile. 'The King is easy to predict: such a display was perfect in taming my enemies and certain to appeal to his sense of humour. Particularly after the show I made of the coat earlier.' He poured himself a cup of wine. 'You disposed of the garment?'

'Yes, Master. I took it to the merchant's house as you ordered.'

'Then you have done well, my little Rabbit.' Thomas told the small lad. 'You can be dismissed; get yourself some ale and food but be quiet about it. See what is being said in the halls and kitchens. From this day forth, you will be my eyes and ears about court. I shall make Henry a great king; his name will be remembered forever.' He waved Osbern away. 'As will mine alongside it.'

'Yes, Lord,' Osbern turned to leave, happy to be dismissed.

'Osbern.'

Thomas called him back just as he reached the door, and the Rabbit turned with wide-eyed innocence fixed upon his face.

'Yes, Lord?'

'The coin the merchant gave you, for my fine scarlet and grey cloak?'

Osbern sighed and took the small purse from his tunic and dropped it into Thomas's outstretched hand. He had hoped that his new master would forget that.

''Twas a good price for a beggar's coat,' he sniffed.

Historical Note.

The story of Thomas Becket's coat and the beggar was first recorded in 1190 by William FitzStephen. Whilst it may be apocryphal, used by Thomas's hagiographers to show the closeness of Henry and Thomas, it has always seemed to me to be the perfect stage-managed display with a ring of truth. The two men were undeniably close in the 1150s, Henry gave his son and heir to his Chancellor as a ward, so there seems little need in inventing such a tale – particularly the detail of the scarlet and grey cloak. Relations would sour dramatically after Thomas was made Archbishop of Canterbury by the King in the 1160s, leading to the infamous murder in the cathedral in 1170.

Interview with Jemahl Evans

Can you tell us a bit about yourself? How long have you been writing and what other jobs have you had?

I'm a history teacher in my other life, although I'm rarely I the classroom these days and mainly do some tutoring for 'A' level students. I've been writing for about six years. I have a series of books set in the Seventeenth and early Eighteenth Centuries that's ongoing and published by Sharpe Books, as well as a trilogy of novellas covering Thomas Becket's career. Before teaching I worked in London doing training and development for corporations like IBM and Cable and Wireless, and then went travelling at the turn of the millennium around Asia.

What is it about the Medieval Period that inspires you?

I've been fascinated by the period ever since I was a child. I was given 'A Children's Illustrated History of the Middle Ages' for Christmas one year; a massive book that I pored over. It is such a very different society from ours, and the medieval mind is so far removed from our modern world. It's also a very long stretch, if you count it from the fall of Rome in the west to the fall of Constantinople, it's a millennium of change. When I went to University, I automatically took medieval as an option for my first degree, and was fortunate to have brilliant tutors in Stephen Church and the late Chris

Harper-Bill. My Master's degree then focussed on poetry as propaganda in the late medieval period. As a kid Ronald Welch's books, particularly Knight Crusader, were read again and again, so the medieval has always been a period that grabbed me as a fiction reader as well as historian.

What inspired you to write this particular story?

It's Thomas's triple anniversary this year. A 1000 years since his birth, 950 years since his death and 900 since the shrine in Canterbury was finished. It felt like a good time to attempt a retelling of the story. I lived in Canterbury for year in my twenties and know the town fairly well which also gave me a bit of impetus whilst writing. Becket himself strikes me as a difficult individual, particularly after his ascension to the Archbishopric. Henry II's behaviour was not so different from other monarchs; his grandfather Henry I had exerted similar control over the English church, and the Holy Roman Emperor was in open war with the Pope when Thomas was killed. The murder on hallowed ground was simply a step too far for medieval society, but Henry initially didn't expect the backlash to be so vicious. I think he was honestly perplexed and confused by his former friend's intransigence, but Thomas's death is a real turning point in the relations between church and state. I wanted to try and capture all of that in my retelling of the history. The changing relationship between the two men in utterly fascinating.

What do you enjoy most about writing?

I love the editing process; the first draft I often find

torturous, but once that is done the editing is the best part. I tend to underwrite bare bones then add layers rather than overwrite and trim down. After that there is a real buzz of seeing people enjoy your work, but I think I'd still be writing even if nobody saw my stories. The whole process is very cathartic, like practicing a piece of music for a performance.

If you were transported back to the time your story is set, who is the first person you would want to talk to and why?

John of Salisbury, a scholar and cleric, a lover of books and fine wines. Frankly the period is brutal and hard compared to modernity, so someone with a sense of humour and access to a wine cellar would be vital. If I had to live in the medieval period, I think a monk's life is probably the safest and most interesting.

If there was one event in the period you could witness (in perfect safety) what would it be?

I'd like to see some of the monks at work illustrating manuscripts or genuine troubadours and jongleurs at the court in Aquitaine. Even if I was safe, I think a medieval battle would be far too gruesome and bloody for my modern sensibilities.

Why do you think readers are still so thirsty for stories from this period?

I think it's very much a form of escapism and the

medieval is a very different period. There are easy and obvious social parallels between the modern world and ancient Rome or the Early Modern period. In the medieval period it is really only the human emotions that are the same. Society, morality, all of these are radically different, but human emotions like love and hate, jealousy and greed still drove us. I can use a story set in the 17th Century England to satirise our modern society (and do), with the medieval it's the human stories that really draw the reader in.

How important is it for you to be part of a community of writers, and why?

I think it's very important. Writers are a solitary breed generally, we have to be to get the stories out, and often friends and family don't quite get that. It's good to be able chat with people who understand where you're coming from in that respect. When I started writing in particular, it was a writer's group that helped me hone and edit before putting my first book in front of publishers. Honest feedback is so difficult to find when you start writing, and other writers understand that and are a generally helpful bunch. I wouldn't have finished that first book without them, and would recommend anyone starting to write to find a group of likeminded people to discuss stuff with. That can be online these days, and there are loads of websites specifically for historical fiction that cater to writers' groups.

Where can readers find out more about your books?

You can follow me on twitter @Temulkar and my website

is https://jemahlevans.wixsite.com/jemahlevans and you can find me on Facebook at https://www.facebook.com/TheLastRoundhead/

A Knight's Tale by Richard Foreman

"Christians, hasten to help your brothers in the East, for they are being attacked. Arm for the rescue of Jerusalem under your captain Christ. Wear his cross as your badge. If you are killed your sins will be pardoned."

Pope Urban II.

***

A chorus of belching, bravado, gossip, curses, dice-throwing and retching noises swirled around the weathered tavern, situated close to the docks in Taranto. The establishment was populated by various tradesmen, sailors, soldiers, and whores. The ale, wine, and a watery stew flowed. A barmaid's rump was slapped by a balding, drunken priest. A merchant haggled with a bored looking harlot, as he angled for a discount. Laughter rang out as the ruddy-faced landlord, Gotto, told a joke about a three-legged donkey, a fishmonger's wife and a blacksmith's rusty poker. Gotto could see the humour in most things. A couple of patrons laughed more than most, hoping that their host might reward them with a complimentary drink. Lamps were lit as the light faded outside.

Such an environment was a home from home for Edward Kemp, a veteran English knight. He downed another ale and nodded to a serving girl to fetch another round of drinks—before yawning and then contributing to the chorus of belching. His leather jerkin was as filthy as the joke Gotto had just told. Patches of grey had started to mark his stubble, beneath a broken nose and red-rimmed eyes. Edward

51

couldn't quite decide if he was war or world weary. He drank too much (although he would argue that he drank just the right amount) and slept too little. The knight had spent over two decades fighting various campaigns across the continent, for various companies. Some led by lions, some by lambs. The cynical soldier had experienced enough of Christendom to know that God was about as real as dragons. Certainly, God and a protective dragon were absent when his parents had been butchered, by a Norman raiding party, during the Harrying of the North. Afterwards, the orphan travelled south to become a stable hand, then squire—and then a sword for hire, as a trained knight.

Edward sat in the corner with his long-term friend and brother-in-arms Owen, a stocky Welsh archer—who could be frequently found with a drink in his hand and a grin on his roguish face. The bowman ran a sharpening stone over an arrowhead, attached to its shaft. The two men had recently been joined by Loffredo of Ravenna, a knight who served in Bohemond of Taranto's company. Edward had previously served in Bohemond's army too. The famed and fearsome Norman prince, who had spent most of his life at war (whether fighting against the Byzantine Empire or his own brother), was keen to recruit the English knight once more. And so he had instructed Loffredo to track down the veteran, "If he's not in one of the taverns in town then he's probably dead in a ditch somewhere," and petition Edward one last time to join them on their armed pilgrimage. To capture Jerusalem.

Edward had already heard the news concerning the historic campaign several times. Soldiers and civilians alike were yammering on about little else. Pope Urban had given a sermon, a call to arms, at Clermont, for the noblemen and knights of Christendom to journey east and liberate Jerusalem from Turkish rule. The borders of the Byzantine Empire were under threat. Urban claimed that the Turkish hordes were moving westward, intent on conquest and enslavement. Turks were reportedly cutting open the bellies of merchants, as they travelled to the Holy City, to steal any coins they may have swallowed. Christians were being forced to convert to a heathen religion—and being disembowelled or burnt alive if they refused. Christian women were being molested and murdered. Even children were being slaughtered. Shrines and churches were being desecrated, smeared with blood. In return for their military service Urban promised the knights and noblemen that their estates would be secure in their absence. They would be granted a remission of sins. There was also the unspoken promise of booty. The pilgrims would be rewarded, in heaven and on earth. Word spread, like wildfire, about the crusade. Powerful magnates such as Raymond of Toulouse and Robert of Flanders committed their armies and resources. A bishop named Adhemar was hailed as the spiritual leader of the endeavour. Edward was far less zealous about the campaign. Should the Byzantine borders be threatened, then let the Byzantines defend them—or pay others to defend them, as they had done so in the past. When the crusaders reached the Levant—*if* they reached the Levant—they would be far from home. It would be difficult to call up reserves or provision themselves. "It was a fool's errand, a holy fool's errand," Edward had remarked to Owen, on more than one occasion.

Loffredo was all too aware of the Englishman's lack of enthusiasm for the venture. He had already mentioned his desire to return to England, not travel further away from the sodden island. Nevertheless, he still delivered his pitch. Bohemond would reward Loffredo if he could succeed in recruiting the doughty knight and skilled archer.

"Pope Urban is offering crusaders a remission on their sins. The Kingdom of Heaven awaits those who will serve the cause," Loffredo proffered. It would be a just war. "Thou shalt kill Muslims," could be considered a new commandment.

"I am more interested in how Bohemond will reward me in this life, than how God will in the next," Edward replied, after taking another swig of his ale, his voice as rough as his stubble. The knight thought how God would not be able to have his accustomed day of rest, given how many sins would be committed by the goodly Christians during the campaign—and he would have to forgive them.

"Bohemond instructed me to say that he is willing to negotiate terms," Loffredo said: "Only mention that I may be prepared to negotiate if you think that our fish isn't biting," the nobleman had briefed his agent.

Edward displayed little interest still in what Loffredo had to say, but the seed of the idea was taking root. For the past five years or so the Englishman had promised himself that his next campaign would be his last. His ambition was to sail back to England and live a quiet, comfortable life. To buy a house and a share in a tavern. He had spilt enough blood over the years, for three lifetimes. He quite literally had the scars to prove it. But as much as the crusade may be a fool's errand, it might be equally unwise to not profit from it. A fool and their money are easily parted. If Bohemond wanted to open-up the purse strings to recruit him, he wasn't about to argue with the magnate. Edward certainly would not be joining the campaign out of a sense of Christian duty. *The Almighty doesn't much care for me—and I don't much care for Him either.* The campaign could just make it to Constantinople and turn back, in all likelihood. The various princes would probably fall out with one other—or run out of food. It could be easy money—which, aside from free money, was the best kind of money. There were worse commanders out there to serve under too, Edward judged. The Norman prince had inherited his father's guile—and knew how to win. Bohemond also knew how sage it was to look after his men off the battlefield, so they would look after him on it.

"Tell Bohemond that I am prepared to listen to any new terms. He can purchase my soul for nothing, but my sword arm doesn't come cheap," the Englishman replied, raising his voice over the increasing din of the tavern. The regulars had started to enter. A trickle became a stream. A few more whores descended the stairs, dressed in cheap jewellery and either cheaper garments. A trio of dockhands, with besmirched faces, ordered the first of many drinks. Edward recognised the men from previous sessions spent in the tavern. The knight expected to see at least one of the dockers asleep in the gutter, in a pool of piss or sick (or both), by the end of the night. A couple of well-built, well-armed figures also entered and sat on adjacent table to Edward. They both glanced around the establishment, decidedly unimpressed and disdainful. Owen thought that they looked like they were sucking on a lemon and chewing a wasp simultaneously. Their complexions were sunburnt and freckled. They shared the same lantern jaw and mane of fire-red hair. They were probably brothers, or at least cousins. They grunted a couple of times, but otherwise spoke quietly to one another.

"I will tell him," Loffredo replied. "I hope you change your mind, Edward. Jerusalem and our Christian brethren need liberating. God wills it. Do you just want to spend your days in run-down taverns, drowning your sorrows and tupping second-rate whores?"

"Aye, I've found my promised land, Loffredo. And I have got nothing against you finding yours, in the desert," the Englishman remarked, good humouredly. Edward offered to buy his fellow knight another drink, but he took his leave. Bohemond had instructed the agent to seek out other soldiers to recruit. To take the cross. To save or damn them.

***

Owen placed a jug of ale on the uneven table and sat down on his even ricketier stool. Before wending his way through the crowd, back to Edward, the archer caught the eye—or she caught his eye—of Maria. The young, but experienced, whore was wearing a red linen dress which tantalisingly hung off her left shoulder—enticingly displaying the promise of her right breast. Owen had already spent two nights with Maria. Ever since she had offered him a small discount after their first encounter, he had become veritably smitten with the lissom, Venetian brunette.

"It looks like I may be joining this crusade, to Jerusalem," the Welshman remarked to Maria, his muscular arm bulging, from holding the large jug of ale. "This might even be the last night I spend in Taranto, for some time."

"Well make sure you spend it with me," Maria replied, before pouting, her voice even sultrier than usual. "I'll ensure that you set off on your campaign with a smile on your face, instead of a pox between your legs—which will happen if you visit the neighbouring brothel. The girls there are unclean. Foreign. I will even give you another discount, because I like you and I may never see you again. We'll have some fun, I promise."

"You've made me an offer I can't refuse. I will see you later in the evening, I promise," Owen assured her, his eyes and other parts of him bulging, before making his way back to the table.

A short silence ensued after the archer sat back down, as both men started to ruminate on the possibility of joining the crusade.

"It seems that Bohemond has become a servant of God," Owen finally, wryly, remarked, arching his eyebrows—a picture of devout scepticism.

"Bohemond probably looked into the possibility that God could become a servant of him first. I will listen to any fresh terms he offers, before making a decision to pledge to the cause," Edward said, responding to his companion's unasked question.

Owen trusted the knight to negotiate his pay too. More than Edward, Owen needed the coin that the crusade could provide. He had experienced too much good living recently, if "good" meant sinful, in the form of gambling, drinking and whoring. The bowman wondered what the women in the East would be like. He had heard a disconcerting rumour that Muslim fillies didn't drink, which would limit the archer's ability to take advantage of them. He worried that there must be a reason why so many women from the East wore veils too. Was it to conceal an ugly truth? He joked to himself that he would aim to bring back a chest of veils for the women of Wales, to make them seem more appealing.

"Our Count of Taranto may well submit to God's will, but I can't envision him taking many orders from fellow mere mortals. He has grown accustomed to being in command, since his father passed," the bowman remarked, whilst keeping half an eye on Maria. She was flirting with a dockhand. He was in his cups—he might soon be in her bed.

"Aye, but the likes of Raymond of Toulouse have grown accustomed to being in command too. I would back Bohemond to be the dog who gets the bone, after any fight, though. The Count of Taranto tends to get what he wants. He's an ambitious bastard. Too ambitious. He won't be happy until he's sitting on a throne somewhere, with no more kingdoms left to conquer. Even then he would find something wrong. His food would be too cold, his wine would be too sour—and his wife would be too faithful," Edward argued, refilling his cup.

"He will surely have to swallow his pride and submit to the will of Emperor Alexios. Not that Alexios would consider himself a mere mortal."

"I suspect that Bohemond will be willing to align himself with the Emperor, right up until the moment when he stabs him in the back. Unless Alexios stabs Bohemond in the back first. At some point the Emperor will regret inviting our paymaster into his alliance—letting the fox into the hen house. Bohemond would happily chew him up—and spit him out. It's natural for a son to want to carry on the war that his father lost, although Robert Guiscard did disinherit Bohemond. Alexius is no longer as strong as he once was. Hence, he needs us to fight his battles for him. The empire is

58

contracting. The Seljuk Turks are a pack of hyenas, bringing down a once mighty lion. Alexios used to be an accomplished general. But court life has made him soft. Rumour has it that he spends more time with his mistresses, than his generals and advisers. He's as pox ridden as a French harlot. He is more likely to raise taxes than morale nowadays. The Byzantines are not known for their loyalty and honour. Alexios will have plenty of close allies, waiting for him to fail. He's just keeping the throne warm for them... The fight has gone out of Komnenos. His eunuchs have bigger bollocks."

The sound of a couple of chairs scraping across the floor drowned out the noise of Owen's laughter. The two hulking figures from the neighbouring table now towered over the Englishman and Welshman. Riled. Glowering.

The atmosphere suddenly changed, as if a chaplain had just extinguished all the candles in his church.

"Curs! Your words are tantamount to blasphemy. You are not even worthy enough to voice the Emperor's sacred name. You would be executed for such calumny and sedition in Constantinople. We are Varangians," the slightly larger of the two men, Gorm, asserted—he widened his nostrils and puffed out his chest whilst pronouncing the name of the Emperor's famed unit of bodyguards.

His companion, Sten, grunted or growled in agreement, his hand clasped around the hilt of a large, curved dagger.

The Varangian Guard. Their reputation preceded them. And was deserved. The ancient group of soldiers was more akin to a cult. Formidable in battle. Fiercely loyal. Their ranks were largely made up of Norsemen, although many Anglo-Saxons migrated to the East and swelled their ranks after William the Conqueror's victory in 1066. Or, as Edward and others called him, William the Bastard. The Varangian Guard seldom recruited soldiers from inside the Empire, to lessen the possibility of corruption and treachery. Few troops could live to tell the tale of standing against the elite soldiers. Their large battle-axes could chop down men, as easily as a gardener can pull up weeds. The Varangians were instrumental in defeating Robert Guiscard's forces, snatching triumph from the jaws of defeat during more than one engagement. Bohemond still cursed the imperial guard whenever their name was mentioned, although his antagonism was tempered with admiration.

The Varangians had been ordered by Tatikios, one of the Emperor's key generals, to travel to Taranto to deliver orders to a Byzantine spy posted there. Tatikios was keen to assess the strength of Bohemond's forces, before they descended upon Constantinople, along with the other crusader armies. Both Gorm and Sten were seemingly in competition with one another, as to who could project the most imperious and contemptuous sneer when looking down at the westerners. They were long time companions, kinsmen from the same tribe. Their fathers had served in Harald Hardrada's army. After Hardrada's defeat at Stamford Bridge, the spearmen had taken their families east. The sons followed in their father's footsteps and served in the Varangian Guard, swearing oaths of allegiance to Alexios Komnenos.

The sight of the Varangians would have intimidated most men. But Edward Kemp wasn't most men. The knight had no desire to enter into a fight with the men in front of him, but he couldn't—wouldn't—withdraw from any encounter either. It was not a question of being brave, rather the

Englishman would not be bullied. He sized up the taller of the two Varangians in front of him. His face was large and brooding, like a bullock's. His chest was as broad as a double-headed axe. If they all drew their blades, blood would be spilt. Lives, as well as pride, were potentially at stake. And victory was far from certain.

Edward calmly got to his feet. Owen stood too. The knight took a swig of his ale and spoke with held his hands up in a conciliatory gesture.

"We meant no offence. Can I buy you both a drink?"

The knight offered an olive branch. But it was snapped in two.

"No. But you can get out of our sight. Leave!" Gorm spat out.

Edward turned to his friend. Owen offered up the subtlest of nods, to convey that he would be ready if things went from bad to worse.

"We will soon be allies, gentlemen, fighting together in the East. We need to learn how to drink together under the same roof."

"We do not need you or Bohemond's army to triumph in the war with the ignoble Turk," Gorm posited, disgusted by the thought of the Varangian Guard despoiling its honour by having to fight alongside the likes of the barbaric English knight in front of him.

"Your precious Emperor has decreed that he needs us— and I thought you considered him infallible, like our venerable Pope Urban," Edward drily replied.

"Our loyalty is to the Emperor and Empire. Your crusader armies and your Pope Urban can go rot. You are English, no? England can go rot too," Gorm argued, bristling, as he echoed the words of his late father in relation to the accursed island.

"I'll drink to that," Owen chirped, smiling as the Welshman raised his cup in a toast.

"Are you mocking us?" the dog-toothed Sten emitted, his voice as rough as granite. The brawny Varangian looked like he wanted to kill the archer. Which he probably did.

"You're doing a great job of mocking yourself. But I'll help you out if you want," the feisty bowman replied. As much as the Emperor's bodyguard were renowned for their sense of honour, their sense of humour was conspicuous by its absence.

Sten let out a grunt cum growl again. The tension in the air increased, like the tightening of a garrotte. The Varangian gripped his dagger even more, pulling the weapon out a little so a slither of the blade was showing.

"I'd leave that dagger in its sheath, if I was you," Edward warned, his voice now as cold, flat and hard as his sword. "You might do yourself an injury. Or rather I'll do you an injury."

Perhaps part of Edward knew that the Varangian's temper would boil over, as oppose to simmer, by issuing the threat.

An indignant Gorm spat out a curse in his native tongue, or an order for his anxious companion to attack. Edward and Owen had participated in more than one tavern brawl over the years. The knight was aware that chivalry had little part to play in proceedings.

Gorm reached for his sword, but as he grabbed the weapon Edward buried his boot into his opponent's groin. Pain clanged upwards through his torso, as if the blow might cleave him apart.

Owen reacted as quickly as his friend—and fought just as dishonourably and desperately. The Welshman first threw the contents of his cup into Sten's face, with his left hand. And with his right he snatched up the arrow he had been sharpening from the table and plunged it into the Varangian's eye. The arrowhead easily pierced through the jelly—and halfway through what little brains the Dane possessed. The high-pitched scream, which sounded like the cry of a eunuch (while he was in the process of becoming a eunuch), sliced through the convivial atmosphere of the establishment. But then the noise subsided, as abruptly as it started.

Gorm staggered backwards, doubled over in agony. Winded. The air rushed out of his lungs, like bellows. Just as he was about to recover—and his fingertips tickled the hilt of his sword—Edward repeated the assault. The dockhands winced, and their eyes nearly watered in sympathy as the blow landed. Gorm's tree trunk-like legs buckled and he fell to the floor, like a drunk. The Englishman towered over the prostrate Varangian. A brace of rats scurried along the floor behind Gorm and disappeared into a V-shaped hole. Edward had no desire to proffer a pithy line—or make a display of triumphalism over his opponent. He took no—or very little—pleasure in killing the Varangian. The Dane drew in a breath and was about to speak. He might have wanted to plead for his life—or condemn the Englishman. Before any words fell from his drooling, twisted mouth, however, the knight stabbed the point of his sword into the Varangian's gullet. He gurgled and writhed for a few moments, then stopped. Tavern brawls could be, like life, nasty, brutish and short. The imperial bodyguard was not the first man Edward had ever killed in such a manner. And he probably wouldn't be the last.

Mouths were agape. Whispers scurried around the tavern like the rats, or like air rushing around the inside of a seashell. Gotto could laugh at most things. But not everything. The landlord pursed his lips, either upset at the needless loss of life—or that he would have to clean up the mess. The Englishman and Welshman drank a lot and were usually no trouble. But (nearly) no amount of money was worth such trouble. Word would spread about the incident faster than a pox spreading at the neighbouring brothel.

Edward could not help but observe the landlord's displeased expression. He would give Gotto some coin by way of an apology for the trouble he had, not caused, but been involved in. His host would be responsible for scrubbing the blood from the warped, wooden floor. But it would ultimately fall to Bohemond to sweep things under the carpet. Edward knew he would be in the prince's debt. And Bohemond knew how the knight would repay him. *The Count of Taranto tends to get what he wants.* The Englishman probably would not be able to now refuse his request to join the foolish campaign. And his bargaining position to negotiate upwards was as dead as the Varangian with blood still pouring out his throat. The knight would still petition for Owen to receive an increase in pay, however.

Edward sighed. He was world and war weary, he realised, as he wiped the blood off his blade—using the Varangian's shirt to do so. It was a shame that he had to kill the man. It was equally a shame that his fine boots were a couple of sizes too big for the knight.

Owen liberated the curved dagger from the corpse at his feet. Not to serve as a trophy, but to sell on and use the money to spend another night with Maria.

"What will happen now?" the archer asked his friend.

The Welshman was going to joke that they could use a remission of sin at present. He was also going to mention how he wanted to test himself against the famed Turkish bowmen in the East.

"God knows," Edward replied, emitting another sigh.

Interview with Richard Foreman

Can you tell us a bit about yourself? How long have you been writing and what other jobs have you had?

I have largely worked in publishing - as a publicist, consultant and publisher - for the past twenty years. "Books are the proper study of mankind," as Aldous Huxley once said. I may have taken that advice a bit too far, however. Life used to be a merry-go-round of book festivals, author drinks and publication dinners. If only my book sales were as high as my cholesterol. The lockdown has definitely helped with productivity and sobriety.

I wrote my first book, *A Hero of Our Time*, in my early twenties - and it shows. But first books should be a learning curve, as one's last book should be a learning curve too.

What is it about the Medieval period that inspires you?

In its power politics, egotistical protagonists, and dramatic narratives the Medieval period resonates and holds a mirror up to aspects of society today. The past isn't dead, it's not even past. Soldiers can still be cruel and Christian. Conquest can be relabelled as colonisation. Leaders have private as well as public agendas. Yet history also fascinates because it can seem so strange and alien. The past is a foreign country. They do things differently there.

The First Crusade produced a legacy, which still echoes in the relationship between the West and Middle East - but regardless of that it is a story about faith, war, human suffering and heroism which would still grip autonomous to its significance in history. The human story of characters, as well as the bigger picture of historical events, needs to inform and inspire any novel.

Thankfully, there are enough sources to shine a light in the darkness of Medieval history - but not too many where one needs to endlessly research things. When writing my first medieval series, Band of Brothers, set during Henry V's Agincourt campaign, I was mindful of trying to capture the humour and humanity (or inhumanity) of the soldiers and noblemen of the time - that there were parallels between Medieval England and England today. Of course, we are no longer at war with France or have a prickly relationship with Scotland, as we did then.

If you were transported back to the time your story is set, who is the first person you would want to talk to and why?

Bishop Adhemar. The first person to take the cross really did hold the crusade together. He was a priest, diplomat and warrior. He comes across as being both pious and urbane. Adhemar seemed to be universally admired by the leading princes of the campaign. Indeed, they probably agreed on little else. When he passed, the frail coalition between the princes began to fall apart. The pilgrims genuinely mourned their spiritual leader and his legacy still influenced proceedings. I am also intrigued by Godfrey of Bouillon.

How much was he genuinely pious and heroic, or how much has he benefitted from some good publicity?

If there was one event in the period you could witness (in perfect safety) what would it be?

Due to my ardent cowardice I would have stood on the ramparts, instead of participating in the fighting, but I would have liked to have witnessed the Battle of Antioch, which features in the second book of series, Besieged. The crusaders had starved and suffered for months yet they mustered themselves and bravely marched out to meet an enemy force over three times their size. Against all odds they triumphed. The victory altered the course of the campaign - and history.

What are you writing at the moment?

The third and final book in the First Crusade series, which is provisionally titled *Jerusalem*. Am just at the stage where I am researching the Siege of Jerusalem and planning story. After that I may return to Ancient Rome and Augustus Caesar, or write another series set during Medieval era. The Third Crusade is a natural follow-up. Am also flirting with writing a book about the Black Prince.

How important is it for you to be part of a community of writers, and why?

There's an understandable bond between writers, because we're in the same trade and can share the same frustrations, gossip and resources. Writing is a largely solitary profession so it's healthy to chat and meet up. Alcohol is a wonderful bond too.

Where can readers find out more about your books?

All my books are on Amazon, including *Siege* and *Besieged,* which *A Knight's Tale* is the precursor to. Although I have largely written series set in Ancient Rome - about Julius Caesar, Augustus and Marcus Aurelius – I have also written books set during WW2 and the Victorian period. I am happy to hear from readers and be contacted via twitter @rforemanauthor or email richard@sharpebooks.com

Should you be a debut or established author and have written historical fiction, set during the Medieval period or otherwise, then I am happy for you to get in touch too about Sharpe Books publishing your titles.

The Quest by Hilary Green

I, Pedros of Antioch, brother infirmarian in the Order of Knights of the Hospital of St John of Jerusalem, take up my pen to record the life and the noble deeds of Ranulph of Erbistock, in the country of England, Knight of this Order, and sometimes known as Ironhand for his prowess with the sword.

It is fitting that first I should introduce myself and explain why I, rather than any other, should be the one to relate this story. I was born, as my name suggests, in the great city of Antioch in the blessed year of Our Lord 1099; doubly blessed because it was in that year that, with God's help, the Christian armies wrested the Holy City of Jerusalem from the grip of the infidel. I grew up in the household of Firouz bin Dmitri, believing myself to be an orphan, the son of Hamid bin Ismael, a Turkish silk merchant, and his wife Mariam. That, in itself, was unusual. Hamid was a Muslim, as you might expect, but Mariam was a Christian, who worshipped in the Armenian doctrine. She was Farouz's sister, which is how I came to be brought up by him after my mother died giving birth to me. In those days, so I have been told, Christians and Muslims lived side by side in Antioch, each tolerating the other's customs and beliefs.

I was not the only one of Mariam's children living in the household. There were also my two older brothers and a sister. Firouz's wife had died young and he had no children of his own, so he behaved to us as if we were his. You might imagine that we were a happy and united family. It was not so – or not at least for me. From my earliest childhood my brothers teased and tormented me. I always felt that I was different from them, though I could not understand why. For one thing, my eyes were blue, while theirs were dark, They made fun of that, saying they could see right through into my brain and know what I was thinking. One of them said once that my eyes were the same colour as the sky reflected in a puddle after rain; so after that they called me 'puddle eyes'. At other times they called me 'cuckoo', though they refused to tell me why. The biggest difference, and one that puzzled me most, was the fact that they were circumcised and I was not. They mocked me for it and I was ashamed to be seen naked. One day I plucked up courage to ask my Uncle Firouz why this was. He patted my shoulder and said, 'That's easily explained. Your mother was a Christian, as am I, and it is not our custom to circumcise our sons. Your brothers were born while Hamid was still alive, so they followed the custom of his people.'

This answered one of my questions, but did not dispel the hostility between me and my brothers. I learned to live with it. It helped that by the age of sixteen I was taller than them and broader in the shoulder. My uncle saw to it that all three of us had a good education and as we grew up he gave each of us a position in his business. My brothers seemed to resent that. They thought that the business should be theirs when our uncle passed away and wanted me to have no share in it. For my own part, I found the life of the counting house stultifying and longed for a chance to leave Antioch and seek wider horizons. I was bored and often scanted my duties, which made them resent me even more. Over time our enmity grew more bitter, until one day it erupted in violence and I found myself on my back with both of them on top of me and a knife at my throat.

The noise had alerted my uncle, who rushed out of his inner office and shouted at them to desist.

'What is going on here?' he demanded. There was no response. 'Well?'

We stood, panting and glowering at each other until my elder brother muttered, 'It's him. He doesn't belong here.'

My uncle looked at us in silence for a moment. Then he said, 'You two older boys, get back to your work. I'll deal with you later. Pedros, come with me.'

He led me out into a courtyard and seated himself under the shade of a palm tree. I stood before him, trembling, wondering what punishment I might expect and trying to stifle my sense of injustice. Why, I asked myself, should I be blamed? What had I ever done to make them hate me?

'Sit, Pedros,' my uncle said. 'I need to talk to you. I should have done it long ago but I kept putting it off, looking for a time when I felt you were ready to hear what I have to say.'

I sat, on the edge of a bench, and clasped my shaking hands between my knees.

'This is a long story I have to tell you,' he began. 'You must listen patiently. In the end you will understand. Many years ago, when I was still a young man, working under my father as you are doing under me now, a merchant came from across the sea. You have seen the great galleys sail into the port of Seleucia, bringing merchants from the west to purchase our silk. This one came in a galley flying the flag of Amalfi. Its master was a man named Ranulf and though his home then was Amalfi he had been born, he told us, much further north and west, in the country of England. He came to my father's shop to buy silk to take back to Italy and though he was a shrewd negotiator he was also fair and my father took a liking to him. He invited him to dine with us and during his time in Antioch we saw a good deal of him. He and I were much of an age and we became friends. He was a comely man, tall and broad shouldered like many of his countrymen, and with hair the colour of spun gold. He was well-read and had travelled widely, and he could converse easily on many subjects and in many languages. I know he spoke at least four. It might have been more.'

I shifted on my seat, beginning to wonder what all this had to do with my fight with my brothers, but my uncle went on: 'Your mother, my sister, was a young girl then but it never occurred to me to consider what impression this stranger might be having on her.' I started and would have interrupted him, but he continued, 'When his business was concluded Ranulph sailed away, but the following summer he came back and this time it was clear that he and Mariam were in love. He went to our father and asked his permission for them to marry, but unbeknown to me father had already agreed with Hamid that Mariam should be his wife. He was a rival in the business of selling silk and a union between the two families made good commercial sense. Mariam wept and begged father on her knees to allow her to marry Ranulph and in the end he yielded and agreed that, when the next sailing season came round, if Ranulph returned and if they were both still of the same mind, he would permit the union.'

I felt my heartbeat quicken. Was I about to learn the secret of the difference between me and my brothers? But as quickly as the idea came to me I dispelled it. All this must have happened many years ago, long before I was born.

My uncle was still speaking. 'All the next summer we waited and watched for a galley with the Amalfitan flag to enter the harbour, but it never came and when winter arrived my father insisted on honouring his promise to Hamid. He and Mariam were married a month later.'

My spirits, which had quickened, flagged again. 'But what had happened?' I asked. 'Why did he not return, as he promised?'

'We did not know. I was convinced that something must have happened to him. I did not believe that he would have changed his mind. In the end we concluded that he must have been killed by pirates, or his ship was sunk in a storm. More summers passed, and we saw no more of him, and in the end we began to forget – well, at least I did.'

'And my mother …?'

'Hamid was a good husband to her. He kept his promise that she should be allowed to continue in her own faith, provided the children were brought up in the faith of Islam. She was not, I think, unhappy. But then …'

'Then?'

'You will know the story of the great siege.'

I fidgeted in my seat. That was ancient history, before I was born. I had never taken much notice of what I was told. 'I know something … not much.'

'The day came when the army of the Franks arrived at our gates. They were going to Jerusalem, to free it from the infidels, but Antioch stood in their way. By then we had a new ruler, Yaghi Siyan, a devout, I would say fanatical, Muslim. The old accord between Christian and Muslim was broken and Yaghi was never going to open the gates to a Christian army. So they sat down outside our walls and laid siege to us. It lasted from October to June the following summer and by then all our stocks of food were used up and we were close to starvation – indeed people were dying, more and more every day. Mind you, the Franks were not in much better condition. They had stripped the surrounding countryside bare and they dare not venture far from the camp because bands of Turkish soldiers were roaming the area. Yaghi had conscripted all men below a certain age, whether Muslim of Christian, to watch the walls. I was one of them, and one day when I was on duty the Franks mounted an attack. It was beaten off but as I looked down from the walls I suddenly saw a face I recognised …'

'It was him!' I broke in, unable to contain myself. 'Ranulph, it was him?'

'Yes, it was and then …'

My uncle stopped suddenly and ran a hand over his face, as if to shut out a memory too painful to be voiced. For a long moment I waited, forcing myself to restrain my impatience. At length he lifted his head and sighed.

'There's no need to go over the details. You know that the siege was broken and the Franks found a way into the city. We had been told … it was said … that Prince Bohemond, who led the attack, had promised that if the gates were opened no Christians would be harmed. But once they were in they slaughtered indiscriminately. Christians and Muslims were cut down, their houses looted, their women raped. Ranulph and I raced to the house where your mother lived with Hamid ….'

'You were with him? You were together?'

'We had … encountered each other. We reached the house in time to prevent the worst of the slaughter, but in the fighting Hamid received a fatal wound. Ranulph was wounded too and we feared for his life, but your mother sent for an old friend, Ibn Butan, the great Arab doctor who had set up a hospital here. He cared for Ranulph's wounds and slowly he recovered. But then, as you will know, we found ourselves once more under siege, this time from a Turkish army under the Emir Kerbogha. That was when a priest who was with the Frankish army claimed that he had discovered the Holy Lance, the lance that pierced the side of Christ as he hung on the cross. The Franks sallied out, with the lance as their banner, and whether it was the power of the holy relic, or simply that they took the Turks by surprise,' the note of irony in my uncle's voice told me which explanation he believed, 'whichever it was, the Turkish forces fled and the Franks were victorious. It was then that your … that Ranulph found in Kerbogha's tent a box of books, many of them medical treatises by some of the great Arab doctors. He brought them back to the city and presented them to Ibn Butan, and after that they spent many hours together. Ranulph had always had an interest in medicine.'

I had the impression that for a while my uncle had not been talking to me, but simply reliving a past that was engraved on his memory. But now he seemed to come to an awareness of his real purpose.

'After the siege was lifted the Franks remained in the city for several months, and during that time Ranulph and your mother renewed their love for one another. They were married a few days before the army left on its way to Jerusalem. They had been gone a month when your mother realised she was with child.'

'So, Ranulph is my father?' I could scarcely draw breath

enough to utter the words.

'Yes. You are the son of Ranulph Ironhand, not Hamid bin Ismael.'

I felt as if a great bubble of pride and relief was expanding inside my chest, until it was burst by a sudden sharp pang of pain. 'Why have I never seen him? Why hasn't he come here to find me? Does he even know I exist?'

My uncle sighed. 'This is why I have never spoken of this to you before. I do not know. I wrote to him, to tell him your mother was with child, but whether or not the letter ever reached him I cannot say. You know that your mother died giving birth to you. You were born much too soon and the midwives declared that there was no hope for you and it was better to let nature take its course. But unknown to me, Ibn Butan took you and gave you to a wet nurse and between them they kept you alive. He said nothing to me until he was sure you would survive. Meanwhile, I wrote again, telling your father that both you and Mariam were dead. When I heard that you were, in fact, alive I wrote again, but I heard nothing in reply. It is not surprising. With an army on the move, or in the heat of battle, it is not likely that letters would reach their intended recipient.'

'And you have never heard from him again?' I asked.

My uncle reached across and laid a hand on my arm. 'I'm sorry, Pedros. I came to the conclusion years ago that he must be dead. If he had survived, and had not received my letters, he would have returned to his wife, of that I am sure. And if he did receive them, he would have come to find you. The only explanation is that somehow, in battle or by one of those sicknesses that haunt army camps, he was killed.' He pressed my arm and repeated softly, 'I am sorry.'

For a long moment we sat in silence. My spirits were like a fallen leaf, blown hither and thither by contrary winds. Should I rejoice that at last knew my true parentage, knew myself the child of a great warrior? Or should I be mourning the loss of the father I had never known?

At length I said, 'Tell me about him?'

My uncle lifted his shoulders. 'There is little more to say, other than what I have told you already. He never spoke much of his childhood or his early years. I had the impression that there were things that happened then that he was reluctant to recall. He did tell me once that he was the son of a nobleman. His father was lord of the village where he was born, until he was killed by the soldiers of William of Normandy when he conquered England. Ranulph was left an orphan, brought up I believe by monks. What happened after that I never knew precisely. I know he was a sailor, and then a mercenary soldier. That was where he earned the name of Ironhand, for his strength and his prowess in battle.' He smiled briefly. 'Mark you, amongst the merchant community he was called Goldenhand, because every deal he undertook seemed to turn to gold. When he became a knight he took that as his device, a mailed fist in a golden glove.'

'Did you ever find out why he did not return to claim my mother's hand?' I asked.

'It was as I guessed. His ship was waylaid by pirates and he was captured, but instead of killing him they sold him into slavery. When he eventually escaped he heard from an old friend that your mother was married, and he thought it better to stay away. If he had not joined the army of Prince Bohemond we should never have seen him again.'

My uncle rose and stretched his arms. 'That is enough for

today. I must go and deal with your brothers – your half-brothers, I should say. There is no need for you to go back to your work. You need time to think. We will talk again tomorrow.'

From that day on I could think of nothing but learning more of this marvellous man whose blood ran in my veins. I haunted the bazaars and inns where merchants gathered, in the hope one of them might have news of him. I went to the schools where the wise men teach and to the priests in our churches, asking if anyone remembered him. A few did, and all spoke well of his learning and his gentle disposition. At the hospital Ibn Butan was long dead but those who had trained under him showed me the books my father had brought from the Turkish camp, and spoke of how greatly they valued them. But no one could give me any news of his ultimate fate.

One day someone said, 'You should seek an audience with Duke Roger. He and your father were comrades in arms. If anyone knows what happened to him, he would.'

Duke Roger of Salerno was ruling Antioch as regent for Prince Bohemond's infant son. I had seen him riding out surrounded by his knights but of course I had never spoke to him. Nevertheless, I could not miss a chance of finding answers to the question that obsessed me, but before I could pluck up my courage the whole city was rocked by the news that the Artuqid ruler of Aleppo, the atabeg Ilghazi, had gathered his forces and attacked some of the towns on the outskirts of the principality of Antioch. It was rumoured that he intended to attack the city itself. Roger called together his knights and rode out to do battle with him. I stood on the walls, with hundreds of my fellow citizens, and watched them leave. At the head of the column Roger was preceded by the great jewelled cross he had taken as his standard. At his side rode the Patriarch of Antioch, accompanied by his attendant priests. Behind them rode a large company of knights, seven hundred of them some said, together with a regiment of Turcopoles, local men who fought as mounted archers. Behind them again marched rank upon rank of infantry, cross-bowmen and pike men. They made a brave sight as they headed away down the road towards Artah on the old Roam road leading towards Aleppo.

A very different sight greeted us a few days later, when the remnants of the army dragged themselves back into the city. They had camped for the night, we heard, in a narrow valley with few routes of escape and in the darkness they had been surrounded by Ilghazi's men. Roger drew up his forces in battle order and for a while it seemed they might prevail but they were outflanked by the Artuqids and Roger himself was killed at the foot of the great, jewelled cross. Of all seven hundred knights, only two survived.

In the days that followed panic gripped the city. At every dawn we expected to see Ilghazi's army marching to encamp around our walls. Suddenly, the old stories of the great siege, which had seemed so irrelevant to me, took on a grim reality. But for reasons we could not understand, they never appeared, though we heard that more of the outlying towns had fallen into their hands. Then came the news that King Baldwin of Jerusalem was coming in person to organise the defence of the city and drive off the Artuqids.

The King arrived with a large force of knights and infantry. The common soldiers made camp outside the walls, while King Baldwin and his knights moved into the castle that dominated the highest point in the city. They were waiting, I heard, for reinforcements to join them from the County of Tripoli and in the interval the memory of what I had intended before Duke Roger left came back to me. Baldwin, I knew, had been with the Frankish army when they marched on Jerusalem. If anyone remembered my father, surely he must. I knew that to ask an audience in the midst of preparations for battle was probably a useless enterprise, but I knew, too, that this might be my only chance to find out the answers to the questions that plagued my waking hours and disturbed my dreams.

Accordingly, I climbed the steep path to the castle. The outer courtyard was busy with all the trades that keep an army supplied. Grooms were rubbing down horses, or holding them while the farrier reshod them. Metal rang on metal and whetstones whined as smiths tightened rivets and sharpened swords. There was a smell of horse dung and hot metal, and through it all the fragrance of freshly baked bread. I made my way into the inner courtyard and found it crowded with other petitioners, all hoping to gain the ear of the king. I threaded my way through them until I was able to catch the eye of one of the stewards.

'Well, what do you want?' he asked, in a tone that already dismissed my request.

I drew a deep breath. 'Please tell the king that the son of Ranulph Ironhand is here and begs a few words with him.'

In a surprisingly short time I was ushered into a large, airy room where Baldwin sat at a table strewn with papers. I bowed and would have knelt but he got up and crossed the room to take hold of me by the shoulders, gazing keenly into my face.

'Ironhand's son, eh? Yes, you have a look of him, about the eyes if nowhere else. I did not know he had a child.'

'I was born after he left for Jerusalem.'

He frowned. 'Surely he must have been told. Has he never returned to find you?'

I shook my head. 'I was not expected to live. If he knew of my birth at all, he must have thought I did not survive.'

He nodded and turned away. 'That explains it. So, what do you want with me? If it's a place in my retinue …'

'No! It's nothing like that.' I swallowed and forced myself to frame the words. 'I just want to know how he died.'

The King turned back to me, his eyebrows raised. 'Oh, dead, is he? It's the first I've heard of it.'

My heart was pounding so hard it was like a drum beating inside my head. 'You mean, he might still be alive?'

'I should be surprised if anything had happened to him and I had not heard about it. We were comrades in arms. He was a formidable warrior for Christ. After we took Jerusalem I lost touch with him, but the last I heard, he had taken Holy Orders and joined the Knights of St John, the Hospitallers as they are called.'

'The Hospitallers...' I repeated. 'I was told he had an interest in medicine …'

'Oh yes. In camp everyone went to him for herbs to cure their ailments. He saved my life once.'

'Do you think,' I asked breathlessly, 'if I went to Jerusalem, to the headquarters of the Hospitallers, they would let me see him?'

'I have no doubt that they would, if he was there, but you may not need to travel so far to find him. Come over here...' He beckoned me to the table, on which was spread a large map. 'See this place here? Zerdana. It's two days ride south-east of here and it is being besieged by Ilghazi, God rot him. I intend to relieve it when we are joined by Count Pons. We shall rendezvous here.' His finger stabbed the map a short distance south of the first place. 'This is the castle of Margat. It was captured some years ago by Tancred, Bohemond's nephew, and he gave it to the Knights of St John to set up a hospital there. I happen to know they are sending a contingent from Jerusalem to join my forces and I should think there is a very good chance your father will be among them.'

I stared at him, unable for a moment to speak. Then I scrambled out the words, 'Can I come with you? I mean, in your train? I'll do anything …'

He looked me up and down. 'You're a well grown lad, broad-shouldered like your father. Have you had any military training?'

I shook my head.

'What do you do? What work?'

'I am a silk merchant.' I had never felt so humbled by my trade.

'Ironhand's son, a silk merchant?' he said. Then, 'But of course, why not? I recall he was a merchant himself before he became a knight.' He looked at me in silence for a moment. 'You'll do anything …?'

'Yes, anything.'

'Very well.' He took up a pen and wrote quickly on a scrap of parchment. 'Give this to the quartermaster. He'll find a job for you. We ride at dawn.'

It must have been a shock to my uncle when I returned to the house and told him what I intended to do, but, by God's grace, he made no attempt to dissuade me. Instead he furnished me with a good horse and a purse of money to cover my necessities while I was away. Next morning, at first light, while I was swallowing a hasty breakfast of a beaker of milk and a few figs, he came to my room. He held out a small box of ebony inlaid with mother of pearl.

'Take this. It was a gift from Prince Bohemond to your father in gratitude for the part he played in raising the great siege. When he left, he gave it to your mother, as a keepsake but also in case of need. I have cared for it since she died, but it is yours by right. Open it.'

I lifted the lid and found, couched on a bed of white silk, a magnificent ruby, set in gold and attached to a golden chain. It was a thing of great beauty and incalculable value.

'Put it on,' my uncle said, 'and keep it hidden under your shirt. If ...when you find your father it will serve, if proof is needed, that you are indeed his son.'

I slipped the chain over my head and tucked the jewel inside my shirt, as he had told me. Against my heart it felt warm, almost like a living thing.

I knelt for my uncle's blessing and then we embraced and I ran down to the courtyard where my horse was waiting, ready saddled. As I reached the gate I turned and looked back. My uncle was standing on the threshold and he raised his hand in farewell. Above him at a window I saw the faces of my two half-brothers and even at that distance I could read the envy in their eyes.

And so I came to the great stronghold of Margat. Having ridden with the quartermaster and his sergeants at the end of the procession it was already thronged with knights and squires, horses and grooms, all wearing the livery of different rulers. I had made it my business on the journey to learn how to recognise the Knights of St John. Their mantles, I knew, were black and emblazoned with a white cross above the heart; but gazing around the crowded outer court I could see no one clothed like that. I took my horse to the horse lines and saw him fed and watered, and then reported to the quartermaster. When he learned that I could read and write he set to work checking lists of stores and it was evening before I was free. I found my way to the inner keep, where many of the knights were gathered and as I looked around my heart gave a sudden jolt. On the far side I saw a group of half a dozen knights in the black mantles of the order, and one of them was half a head taller than the rest. He wore no helm and his hair was dusty from the road, but there was no doubt that is was lighter coloured than any of his companions.

I caught the sleeve of a passing squire. 'Forgive me. Do you know Sir Ranulph, the one they call Ironhand?'

He looked at me as if I was simple. 'Of course. Everyone knows Ironhand.' He jerked his head towards the knights in black. 'Over there. The tall one.'

I stood staring, my heart thudding. I had thought that once I found him I would throw myself at his feet and claim him as my father, but now I was suddenly afraid. Suppose he refused to recognise me? He was a knight in Holy Orders. A son of whose very existence he was ignorant, might be an embarrassment to him. And he stood now among his fellow knights. Surely, I argued with myself, it would be better if I could find a moment when he was alone.

All that evening I waited and watched, but no opportunity presented itself. Then word went round the camp that at dawn next day the army was to advance towards Zerdana. The quartermaster and his assistants, I was told, were to remain at Margat.

Disconsolate, I wandered the halls and passageways of the castle until I found myself in a large hall that had been prepared as a hospital. Most of the pallets were empty, ready to receive the wounded, and none of the infirmarians were present, but close to the door one young man lay, flushed with fever. Seeing me hovering nearby he called out to me, begging for water. I found a jug and some beakers on a table and took him some, raising his head so he could drink. Then, as I laid him back on the pillow and straightened up, I saw hanging from a hook nearby, the tabard that marked him as a lay brother of the order. Glancing down, I knew that there was no chance that he might ride with the others the next day. I unhooked the tabard and slipped it over my clothes.

Next day, in the general melée of departure, no one questioned my presence and I rode out in the train of the Hospitallers. We were heading for Zerdana, but at midday we halted at an oasis I learned was called Tell Danith to water the horses and refill our own flasks. While we were there a horseman arrived on a lathered steed and spoke urgently to King Baldwin. Soon fresh orders were passed along the column. Zerdana had fallen, and we were to fall back on the fortress of Hab, some five leagues to the south.. We camped for the night at the oasis and the following morning the King set out the order for our retreat. Three squadrons of knights headed the column, with the infantry following. A contingent from Tripoli guarded the left flank and another of knights assembled from Antioch held the right. The Hospitallers, together with King Baldwin's own men, were in the centre.

In this manner we began to move towards Hab but before we reached it the Artuqid forces had caught up with us. Their horse archers rode up and down along our ranks, harassing us with a shower of arrows. The knights in the vanguard were forced to disperse and the infantry were drawn up in a defensive formation while battle raged on both flanks. Unarmed and without protection I saw myself being cut down or pierced by an arrow at any moment. Then I saw that some others among the non-combatant followers of the army had retreated to the top of a small hill nearby. I rode after them and from there watched the battle unfold below me.

Interview with Hilary Green

How long have you been writing and what other jobs have you had?

I think I have always written. As a child I was always telling myself stories. I began working seriously in my twenties, when I wrote the first draft of what is now *The Last Hero*. I had been inspired by Mary Renault's novels about ancient Greece and that started me researching the truth behind the myths. *The Last Hero* tells the story of the final collapse of the Mycenenean Empire through the eyes of Alkmaion, the son of the last king of Pylos. It's available on Amazon.

For many years I worked as a teacher. I trained for the theatre at the Rose Bruford College and I taught Drama and Theatre Arts at various schools in London and then on the Wirral, finishing as Director of Drama at the Sixth Form College in Birkenhead. I also ran my own Youth Theatre Company in Epsom, Surrey.

The next novel I wrote was published by Hale and was followed by two short thrillers. They soon went out of print but have now been republished by Sharpe Books, under the titles *State Of Emergency; Codename Omega* and *Operation Omega*.

My real breakthrough came in 2002 when Hodder and Stoughton bought *We'll Meet Again* and *Never Say Goodbye,* two World War II stories. They were followed by the four books in the *Follies* series. Since then I have had three WWI novels published by Severn House and three others by Hale, again. I was then commissioned by Penguin to write four books set in the Victorian period based around children who grew up in the workhouse on Brownlow Hill in Liverpool. These were written under my pen name Holly Green.(The WWI books are now available as paper backs, republished by Penguin in the *Frontline Nurses* series)

What is it about the Medieval period that inspires you?

I have been fascinated by medieval history since studying it for A Level. Initially it was the romantic, swashbuckling stories that I loved but now I am more interested in the way the events and personalities of the era have influenced the way we live today. This came home to me very strongly when I was researching my novel *Ironhand*. The hero of the story, Ranulph, after a period as a mercenary soldier, becomes a successful merchant and as I read I realised that it was trade, far more than wars or crusades, that shaped the world we now inhabit. Anyone who has watched the Netflix series about the Medici will know that their wealth initially came from the manufacture of high quality woollen cloth, the raw material for which was the wool of English sheep, the best in the world. To buy this they needed to be able to transfer large sums of money, so this resulted in the introduction of letters of credit and loans, the foundation of the banking system. This made the Medici and other like them very rich, which enabled them to become patrons or artists like Botticelli and Leonardo da Vinci. It also enabled them to buy luxury items like silk from China and spices from the east. Merchants trading in those commodities came into contact with the Arabic speaking Muslim world. The Arabs had preserved and developed the learning of the ancient Greeks and were streets ahead of the west in mathematics and astronomy and medicine. Western European scholars followed the merchants and began to translate their work. The Arabs had adopted the use of paper from the Chinese and when the printing press was invented all this knowledge became available to a newly literate society. The result was the explosion of the arts and sciences we now call the Renaissance. And all down to the wool from the sheep grazing on monastic lands in Yorkshire and the Welsh Marches!

What inspired you to write this particular story?

This story looks at an aspect of *God's Warrior,* the sequel to *Ironhand*, which is only touched on in the novel. When Ranulph answers the call to join the First Crusade he is instrumental in breaking the siege of Antioch. In the city he finds Mariam, the woman he fell in love with as a merchant and would have married, but for a cruel twist of fate. Their love is rekindled and they marry, but Ranulph has to fulfil his vows as a crusader and leaves for Jerusalem, unaware that Mariam is pregnant. *The Quest* introduces her child, Pedros, and tells how he discovers the true identity of this father and of his quest to find him and receive a father's blessing.

What do I enjoy about writing?

I suppose it's the chance to make something concrete out

of all the ideas and images that are constantly floating around in my head.

If I was transported back to that period who is the first person I would want to talk to and why?

I should like to interview Bishop Adhemar and ask him if he really believed that the shard of metal unearthed in the chapel in Antioch was the remains of the Holy Lance which stabbed Christ on the cross, or whether he just thought it would be a good way of putting heart into the crusaders.

If there was one event I could witness what would it be?

I should like to witness the battle that followed that event in which the crusaders, starving and exhausted, put to flight the forces of the Turks under Kerbogha.

Why do you think people are still so thirsty for stories from this period?

I think people are fascinated by this era for the same reasons I found it so interesting to write about. The characters are so vivid and the events are so dramatic they grip our imagination. At first sight it seems so alien to the way we see the world today, but it has left a legacy, both for good and for ill, that we are still living with.

What are you writing at the moment?

I have just finished the first piece of non-fiction I have ever undertaken. I wrote about my research into trade as an article for Historia. Someone from Amberley Press read it and asked if I would turn it into a book. *Trade In The Middle Ages* will be published in November. Currently I am having a fallow period. I have ideas both for a third volume to follow *God's Warrior* and for books set in World war II and the late Victorian era. Which ideas come to fruition will depend on whether I can find a publisher who is interested.

How important is it for you to be part of a community of writers?

Writing is a lonely business and it's great to be in touch with other people who are engaged in the same endeavour and struggling with the same problems.

Readers can find out more by going to my website www.hilarygreen.co.uk.

Guile by J.A. Ironside

Durham
September 1385

Gregory Maudesley, first Baron of Wynnstree, loyal knight of King Richard II and all round misanthrope, yanked his head back from the cott window and shoved the shutter into place. Half a second later his swift action was rewarded by the *thunk thunk thunk* of three arrowheads embedding themselves in the wood, instead of his skull. The third arrow actually splintered the wood and half emerged through the shutter.

"They're still out there, then?" Ghent said, idly tested the edge of his knife with the pad of a forefinger.

Gregory shot the young knight a sour look. "Why don't you play look-out next time?"

"I suppose I'd present a smaller target." Ghent grinned slyly. "Not to mention a prettier one."

Gregory snorted. He towered over most men by at least half a foot, more if they weren't tall to begin with, and his breadth was in proportion to his height. Perhaps there was some truth in Ghent's suggestion that Gregory was an easy target – he had plenty of scars as evidence. In contrast, Sir Bartholomew Ghent was reckoned to be the picture of handsome knighthood, with the fashionable manners and quicksilver tongue to match.

"Remind me why I don't just throw you out for the Scots to play with?"

"Perhaps because you're going to need someone who's handy with a sword in the very near future?" Ghent glanced at the shutter, which shuddered under the blow of another arrow. "I thought the Scots were no great bowmen."

"They can shoot as well as an English or Welshman. They're just not good at leveraging the ability during battle," Gregory replied. They needed to get out of here. Fall back and regroup with the rest of his men.

"All evidence to the contrary," Ghent said, as the shutter trembled again.

Gregory's mouth pulled into a flat line. "The French appear to be much better at deploying archers." A flash of brightness leapt against the ruined shutter, hot and radiant against the cool night. The first warning scents of smoke curled through the room. "Bollocks in hell!"

"They've set the thatch alight," Ghent said, sounding alarmed for the first time.

"I hate it when they try to burn me alive," Gregory muttered. "Out through the back. Head for the church. Stop for no one. Let's see if you can swing your sword as fast as you can flap your jaw."

They stood by the rear door, swords drawn, snapping the visors of their helmets down. Gregory chose his moment, then charged, bellowing, out into the fire-lit chaos of a Scottish border raid. There were only two men anywhere the door and they were both facing the wrong way. French, judging from the armour. Perhaps they had not thought anyone who might truly pose a threat was inside such a mean dwelling. Gregory took the nearest man down with a blow that cleaved through the meat between neck and shoulder before the luckless soldier had fully turned to face him. A grunt and a limp, wet thud told him that Ghent had disposed of his own target with as little fanfare.

They pelted into the thickening smoke, feet squelching in the mud, while fires gathered strength and sent leaping, demonic shadows through the narrow streets. The people of this suburb appeared to have abandoned it before the Scottish-French army arrived, fortunately for them. With luck, the Scots would employ their usual smash and grab tactics before returning across the border. Gregory had other matters to concern him.

Figures loomed ahead, indistinct in the smoke. Gregory signalled to Ghent and they turned sharply to the left, following the narrow cut between the houses until it opened on to the edge of a churchyard. They crept around the edge of the church, finding the small south door of the transept damaged but negotiable.

Entering the church, Gregory found himself suddenly nose to blade tip, and then Cuthbert lowered his dagger with a jubilant cry of "My lord!"

Muscles in Gregory's back he had not even realised were locked, relaxed. "Young fool! Don't try to hold up a man in full armour with a piddly little knife."

Cuthbert was unruffled by his master's tone. "Better distance to stab him from if he turned out to be French." He grinned, the unloveliness of his crooked teeth, bulbous eyes and lanky, half grown frame somehow completely overshadowed by the expression, so that he looked momentarily angelic.

"Less talk, lad. Put your back into it and help us barricade the door."

Gregory gestured to Ghent who sighed but also picked up

the end of one of the wooden pews. Even with the door barred, their shelter was temporary. The only benefit was that St Giles' appeared to have been looted already, so with luck they would have time to come up with a plan before the marauders returned.

He found to his relief, that Johnson and Rollo were not only alive, but had blocked the main entrance into the church. It was best not to show too much favouritism as a lord but both men were solid, reliable, career men-at-arms. They were completely unalike in all respects – Rollo narrow, lean and laconic; Johnson tall, broad and verbose – save in their loyalty to Gregory. He was glad to have them with him. Of the rest of the party, five of the six men had managed to make it to St Giles. Gregory spared a momentary thought for the poor sod now lost amongst the chaos outside, before setting men to watch while he discussed options with the others. It was supposed to have been a simple mission; track, locate and deliver a message to the king's half-brother, John Holland. But of course the hot-headed fool had fled straight in the direction of the marauding Scots.

Nothing was ever simple.

Gregory signalled Ghent to join the others, after a moment he called Cuthbert over too. The boy might only be sixteen and along as a servant rather than a man-at-arms, but he had surprising insights at times. Gregory was prepared to hear any idea that would get them out of this mess.

***

It had started with an ill-advised campaign in Scotland. The king was almost eighteen-years-old and had no notable battle credits to his name. When France renewed its alliance with Scotland, it had seemed the perfect time for Richard to display a hitherto unseen gift for command, not least since it would make the older, more discontent members of the court more sanguine in his rulership. The king's uncle, John of Gaunt, had been in favour of a campaign in France but parliament had refused to fund such an excursion. When a sizeable French army, led by the chevalier Jean de Vienne, had arrived in Scotland, the plan had changed to the raising of an English army which would engage the Scots in battle on their own land.

It had not gone well.

In hindsight, Gregory thought His Grace, the Duke of Lancaster, ought to have known better than to go along with the scheme since he had led a failed incursion in Scotland only the year before. Perhaps the king had intended the invasion of an English army, fourteen thousand strong, as a *chevauchée* – a punitive march to demonstrate to the Scots the consequences of them being but poor keepers of the treaty. Or perhaps it was to impress upon them the importance of signing a new treaty once the previous one expired. Whatever the reasoning, the Scots responded to the invasion in their time honoured fashion. They declined to engage with the far larger army and disappeared into the highlands, scorching the earth as they went and leaving nothing for the English army to forage.

After less than two weeks of starving in Edinburgh, Richard declared that they would return to England. Gregory suspected that the young king's heart had not really been in the endeavour, some of which could be laid at his half-brother's door.

On the way to Scotland, John Holland had murdered Richard's close friend, Sir Ralph Stafford. No one quite knew what had caused the altercation and Holland had fled before the king's justice could catch up with him. Richard had been equal parts bereft and enraged, cursing his half-brother for a common murderer, and confiscating all his properties and titles. But the damage was done. When the English army finally arrived in Scotland, it was divided and ill-led, with far more violent quarrelling occurring between different houses and allegiances, than between the English and the Scots.

The final straw had been word of the death of the Princess of Wales, Richard's mother. Those who liked to embellish a tale said she had died of a broken heart due to the rift between two of her sons. Gregory, who had met the king's mother on several occasions, found such fancies laughable. If the Princess of Wales had such a prosaic organ as a heart, he was fairly certain it was made of equal parts of granite and steel. Her death was one more blow than the young king could sustain, however, especially in the face of bickering captains, few successes on campaign and a hungry army that was about to turn on itself.

Gregory had thought that was the end of the matter until Richard had summoned him.

"I require you to find my brother, Maudesley," Richard had said. "Take what men you need, but be sure you may trust them."

Gregory had taken this to mean 'be sure none of them have particular ties to any of the feuding factions'. "As you will, Sire. What would you have me do when I find him?"

Richard's dark, clever gaze had been full of conflict as it met Gregory's. "I wish you to deliver a message and then bring him home."

"To face justice?"

"To see about repairing the breach between us," Richard had said. "I do not know if I can forgive him but for the sake of our dead mother, he must be heard and if necessary tried as his station demands."

Gregory had not protested that as a baron, he was no mere messenger. His concerns had lain elsewhere. "I am not the most likely choice for this task, Your Majesty. In truth, I'm as likely to offend your brother as to persuade him."

Richard had smiled then, one of his peculiar, sharp, secret smiles. "That, Maudesley, is why he will believe me to be in earnest."

What Gregory and his men lacked in polish and fashionable manners, they more than made up for in efficiency. Gregory had lived as a mercenary for ten years before inheriting his father's *demesne*, and was used to applying skills few other nobles ever had to acquire. Holland, hearing word that 'the king's dog' was following him, had led them on a merry dance but had miscalculated in flirting with Scottish army. Somewhere in this benighted and burning bishopric, the king's half-brother was hiding from the raiders, well aware that his danger from Gregory was nothing to the danger he faced from the Scots. Holland would be a valuable hostage indeed. The Scots might be able to rebuild half of Edinburgh with his ransom.

***

"Way I see it," Rollo said, "escaping is less of a problem than completing the mission."

"How exactly do you suggest we find Holland in the middle of a raid?" Ghent said. "Perhaps we might all go and stand in the smoke and call his name. Whoever he goes to, is permitted to keep him."

"Doubt the king's brother would thank you for being compared to a stray cur," Rollo said, without rancour. He seemed not to resent the young knight's sarcasm. Gregory had never seen Rollo lose his temper; the man merely killed whoever needed killing and moved calmly on. It was a little unnerving.

"My lord," Cuthbert began, then wilted under the glare Ghent levelled at him.

"Go on," Gregory said.

"We're desperate enough to take the advice of servants now, are we?" Ghent muttered.

Gregory turned to the younger knight, hands curled into fists, expression dangerously pleasant. "If you've nothing more useful to add Sir Ghent, take a turn on watch. Perhaps the man who replaces you will have more to contribute."

Ghent's mouth fell open as he looked from Gregory to Cuthbert and back. "Yes, my lord." His jaw clenched and walked away.

Gregory bit back his exasperation and ignored the curious glances of the other men. "Go on, Cuthbert."

The boy swallowed. "It's only that we know the king's brother was meant to be staying at *The White Horse*. So if it's only that we need to get there, retrieve him and leave, we can do it, I reckon. The inn's only about a mile away."

"But?" Gregory prompted. Normally he couldn't get Cuthbert to shut up. Despite earning out his indenture and being presented with arms two years ago, however, Cuthbert was clearly shy of being too outspoken before so many qualified men-at-arms.

"Is his lordship likely to have noticed the raid and stayed

put, knowing he'd be a target because of his value as a hostage?" Cuthbert said.

"Holland has a vile temper," Johnson snorted. "He's managed to pick fights with far less cause. The boy's right, my lord. If we go to *the White Horse*, we're as like to find that Holland has charged half the Scottish-French army in a rage."

"Reckon we go to the inn anyway," Rollo said. "We need to know for certain."

"If his lordship's been captured, they might not know who he is yet," Cuthbert said. "Maybe we could free him with no one the wiser?"

The man Ghent had relieved arrived then and Gregory questioned him about the direction of the violence. It seemed the army was sweeping east, which gave them a small window of time during which to reach the inn and find out what had happened. Gregory ordered his men into two groups. They were to make their way as stealthily as possible, only fighting if there was no other option.

"Try not to die," Gregory added. "I hate having to find replacements."

Johnson grinned.

***

A half-full ale jug hurtled out of the gloom. Gregory ducked just in time and it struck the door post, the earthenware shattering and scattering pale brown droplets. He was starting to get fed up of missiles of varying types being aimed at his head.

"We intend no harm," he called, trying for a soothing cadence and failing utterly.

"A likely story! Great, scarred brute like you!" A broad,

101

amply padded woman with the sort of arms you'd expect on someone who spent much of their time shifting barrels of ale and knocking drunken heads together, appeared behind the bar. She hefted another jug and let it fly. "Piss off! There's nothing left to steal!"

Gregory and Ghent only just managed to dive out of the way. Her aim was terrifying.

"Truly, Mistress Innkeep, we only want to ask a few questions," Ghent gasped out the words in between several bouts of ducking and weaving, as tankards and mugs filled the air. His usual charm failed to find its mark with the enraged proprietress.

"We don't have time for this," Johnson grumbled.

At the sight of yet another huge man trying to make his way into her inn, the woman let out a shriek of rage, taking up a wicked looking butcher's knife in one hand and a cudgel in the other. Gregory was just considering making a dive for her, hoping that the shock of the attack wouldn't give her time to stab him before he disarmed her, when Cuthbert bobbed up from behind an overturned table.

"We're not Scots. Or French," he said. "We're English. The king sent us."

The woman frowned but the knife in her hand lowered a quarter inch. "The king?"

"We're looking for someone," Cuthbert went on. "That's my master, Baron Maudesley of Essex."

Whether it was because Cuthbert was still only a boy or because he simply had the gift of making people trust him, even like him on short acquaintance, the woman looked at Gregory again. Whatever she saw convinced her he was no Scot. An expression of horror crossed her face and she set the knife down, bobbing a quick a bow.

"My lord...forgive my hasty actions."

Gregory waved her apology off. "We gave you a fright. Answer a few questions and we'll not trouble you further."

She nodded, glaring sideways at Ghent as he helped himself to an unbroken jug of ale but not protesting. "How may I serve you, my lord?"

"You had a noble guest staying here," Gregory said. "I have been sent with a message for him."

"I know who you mean, lord baron, but I'm sorry to tell you that he's gone." Her manner was deferential but she met his gaze squarely. "You can see from the state of the place that the Scots have been through here. Took everything they could carry. I told his lordship to hide. Next thing I know, he's charging down the stairs in his nightshirt, waving a dagger about."

"Was he killed?" Ghent demanded.

The innkeeper gave him a look of supreme disdain. "No. He was taken prisoner. Maybe one of those ruffians recognised him."

"That's it then," Johnson said unhelpfully.

Gregory swore under his breath, temples pounding with fury. The stupid young hothead. First murdering the king's companion, then leading them across half Christendom instead of waiting to hear what they'd been sent to say. And now, when he had an opportunity to hide, Holland had thrown himself into a fight he could not win and got himself taken hostage. The king was not going to be pleased.

"When did this happen?" Gregory said.

"Happen, a half hour or so," the woman replied.

"My lord, we may still have time," Cuthbert said,

bubbling with enthusiasm once more.

"Move out," Gregory told his men. "Ghent make sure you pay for that ale." He tossed a coin to the innkeeper. "For your trouble."

They didn't stay to hear her thanks.

***

In the end, the plan was simple. They watched from a distance as prisoners were lined up so the Scots and French could see who they'd caught. Cuthbert, playing the part of a groom, had managed to get close enough to the prisoners to identify Holland and pass on a short message. On no account was he to admit to his birth, name or station. Instead, he should play the fool. Gregory suppressed a pang of anxiety until Cuthbert returned, affirming that he had delivered the message, although he wasn't certain just how much Holland intended to comply. They would just have to try anyway, Gregory decided.

"There's one other thing, my lord," Cuthbert said. "I heard some of the other servants talking. The Warden of West March is one of the commanders."

Gregory groaned.

"West March?" Ghent said. "Isn't that Archibald Douglas' seat?"

"The very same." Gregory glared. "Alienor is not going to be best pleased."

"So it *is* your wife's father leading this border raid?" Ghent needled.

"It would appear so," Gregory said morosely. "Let's hope this doesn't disintegrate into violence." He did not relish the thought of having to explain to his wife that he'd been forced to kill her father, even if Alienor – who didn't have a good thing to say about the man – probably wouldn't be terribly distressed by such a turn of events.

"If it does, he's as likely to kill you, Maudesley," Ghent said. "I imagine a man doesn't earn the name 'Archibald the Grim' without being a ruthless customer. You may have met your match."

"I'd appreciate you not taking such obvious delight in my impending demise," Gregory said drily.

"Could this be turned to good account?" Rollo mused. "If he's kin, he might be more willing to see you, my lord."

"Spoken like a man without a father-in-law." Ghent laughed harshly.

Privately, Gregory agreed with Ghent. Everything he'd heard about Alienor's father suggested the man was shrewd, ruthless and calculating. A man did not go from dubious beginnings to becoming one of the wealthiest, most influential and powerful landowners in Scotland by being pleasant.

"We cannot leave until we've at least tried to regain Holland," Gregory said. And so they went ahead with their plan.

Gregory was not a man given to nervous attacks, but he felt a hint of trepidation as he entered the Archibald's presence. He had never intended to meet his father-in-law at all and certainly not under these circumstances. The Scottish-French army had taken up temporary quarters in the bishop's palace, near the Cathedral of the Blessed Virgin and St Cuthbert – where the bones of the latter lay entombed.

Archibald Douglas did not rise when Gregory was shown in, trailing Cuthbert walking at a respectful distance, and a disarmed and therefore grumpy, Bartholomew Ghent. He eyed Gregory speculatively. It reminded the knight sharply of the way Alienor looked at a person she was sizing up. In his turn, Gregory took the measure of his father-in-law, searching for likenesses with his wife. Archibald the Grim had the same dark hair and quick, direct gaze as his daughter, but there the similarities ended. He was a big man – nearly as big as Gregory himself – with a face and figure made for war rather than poetry and tourneys. Gregory had heard that Black Archibald had been accused of being a cook's son; that he was a changeling hence his saturnine looks and occasional bouts of strategic cruelty. Gregory's overriding impression was that here sat a man, well into his middle years, who was not done yet. Whose ambition and intelligence would carry him further as long as his frame would allow it. Middle aged or no, Archibald appeared to be in dangerously good physical condition.

"You'll take some wine?" Archibald said, lowland Scottish accent making the words deceptively soft. "Or you'd prefer a dram of *uisge beatha*?"

"Wine. My thanks." Gregory took a seat where Archibald indicated. Ghent and Cuthbert were left to stand.

"You're a long way from home, Baron Maudesley," Archibald commented.

Gregory sipped the wine. Excellent stuff – no doubt from the bishop's private store. "So are you, my lord."

"Merely passing through." Archibald's dark eyes gleamed and Gregory realised the man was enjoying himself. "But your business is more urgent, I understand?"

"The king sent me to perform commissions on his behalf, which is how I find myself in Durham. I am troubling you now because I have reason to suspect that you're holding one of my servants under the misapprehension that he's a man of greater consequence," Gregory said.

"And you would like this servant back?" Archibald said.

Gregory strongly suspected that the March Lord was playing with him. "Yes, my lord."

"It's strange that a servant of yours should stray into our net. I understood Wynnstree to be in Essex. Do you normally allow your servants to roam so freely?" Archibald's gaze flicked first to Cuthbert then to Ghent.

"I didn't say he was a good servant," Gregory said, then cursed himself for picking holes in his own logic.

"I'm surprised you want him back in that case."

"I can't beat a better standard of work into him if you take him back to Scotland." Gregory reached for a callous tone.

Archibald raised an eyebrow. "You're willing to pay a servant's ransom in order to retrieve a man for chastisement? He must have displeased you gravely, Baron Maudesley."

"You can have no idea," Gregory said feelingly. He wished it was possible to beat some sense into John Holland. And he wished that Archibald did not have the same knack for destroying an opponent in conversation that Alienor had. He'd forgotten how thoroughly uncomfortable it was to be on the receiving end of such tactics. Alienor's thorns had been trimmed by affection, with her husband at least.

"I suppose we can come to some arrangement," Archibald said, with the lazy menace of a lounging tiger. "Say eighty shillings in ransom. A fair price for a servant, I think?"

Gregory ground his teeth. It was a steep sum, even if he would insist on Holland returning it to him later. "That sounds reasonable."

"Then we'll go, by and by, and view the prisoners. If you

can pick out the man in question and provide witnesses that he is as you say, there should be no trouble." Archibald smiled to himself. "Of course if he's claimed greater importance than he's entitled to, we'll not be letting him go."

Gregory sincerely hoped Holland had kept his mouth shut.

"You've time for a tale while we drink our wine, I trust?" Archibald said.

"Yes, though I'm no storyteller." Gregory would much rather have abandoned the wine, collected Holland and been on his way. He knew from his wife, however, that amongst the Scots, refusing a tale was a grave insult.

"I shall tell it," Archibald said. "Did you know that when I was a lad, I fought at the battle of Poitiers? I fought on the side of the French of course."

Gregory did not seem to be required to speak so he stayed silent. He heard Ghent shifting restlessly from foot to foot behind him.

"I was captured and taken hostage by the English, Baron Maudesley. Not a grand start to a military career." That elliptical smile again. "Do you know how I was won free?"

"No, my lord." A sinking sensation yawed in Gregory's gut.

"Aye well, Sir William Ramsey, who was likewise a prisoner of the English, started a hue and cry. He accused me of theft. Said I'd stolen his cousin's armour. He cuffed me up and down the enemy lines, forcing me to shed it. He took my shoes. And when a guard said I was the son of a laird and should be respected, Ramsey angrily told the man I was a mere scullion and not worth the trouble of binding. He paid forty shillings for my release and sent me out into the ruined field, where the dead of battle still lay, with a boot up my arse." An almost fond light entered Archibald's eyes. "And so he tricked the great ransom I'd have brought out of English hands."

Gregory felt as if his expression was carved out of granite. The bastard knew. He'd been toying with his son-in-law. "That's quite a tale, my lord."

"Isn't it?" Archibald said affably. "Do you know why I told you this tale?"

Gregory shook his head. It was useless to pretend further. The Scot held all the advantage.

"I have a strong conviction that there should be balance, at least if a man wants his course to run smooth. I paid Ramsey back in coin and in favours. But it was a good deed and that's not so easily redressed." He set his goblet down and rose. "Now I'm the one holding the life of another, potentially valuable man. I see a chance for balancing the scales here. But, Maudesley, be you wed to my daughter or no, I expect debts to me to be paid."

Gregory had also stood up. "What is the price of your assistance?"

Archibald glared at him. "I do a good deed in return for the one I benefitted from. There's no *price*. But one day, I may ask a favour." He moved in on Gregory so they were almost nose to nose. "And when that day comes, Maudesley, you'll be glad to do that favour."

"An it threaten neither my family, my honour nor my king, no doubt I will." Gregory matched him glare for glare.

Archibald chuckled. "Good enough."

***

Gregory's party left Durham the following morning. John Holland rode in the midst of them, happy enough to return to

London having experienced the contrast of Scottish hospitality. He had managed not to state his name and lineage for all and sundry to hear, so when Archibald Douglas told his co-leaders that the man was of no consequence and would be released into the keeping of his daughter's husband, they were willing to let Holland go. Gregory chose not to dwell on any future favours his father-in-law might require. At present, it was a small price to pay for returning the king's half-brother and ending the current round of squabbles between noble houses.

There was nothing they could do about the border raids and he was certain that by the time the English March Lords arrived, the Scots would be back in Scotland, followed by the increasingly disgruntled French forces. Cuthbert had overheard a few French soldiers talking to their Scottish comrades. From what the boy had been able to glean, the French had not stopped complaining – about the barbarism of their hosts, the quality of the food, the lack of wine, the weather – since they had arrived. It was not an alliance that promised a permanent army of the two peoples. In time, the Scots would no doubt sign a new treaty and everyone would go back to raiding each other's borders and stealing each other's sheep and cattle as they had for the last few hundred years.

"I'm still not sure how you pulled that off, Maudesley," Ghent commented. "Did he take a liking to you?"

Gregory snorted. "Nothing so ridiculous."

"What then?"

"Archibald the Grim believes in investing in the future and is keen to have potential allies in many kingdoms."

At least Gregory thought that's what had happened. He

supposed Archibald had not desperately needed the money the ransom of the king's brother would have brought. He suspected Alienor would have greater insights into her father's motives.

For now, it was enough to be going home.

Interview with J. A. Ironside

Can you tell us a bit about yourself? How long have you been writing and what other jobs have you had?

I've been writing professionally for the last seven years, and sneakily for decades before that. Currently I work in a library but I've had a variety of other jobs, most of which were based in the NHS. I also teach self-defence classes and martial arts.

What is it about the Medieval Period that inspires you?

This might sound strange but I'm drawn to the medieval era by the mind-set and by the widespread misapprehensions about medieval life. In many respects, medieval people simply didn't think in the same way a modern contemporary would. However, that mind-set had a logic and evolved amongst social pressures that would leave a modern person completely adrift. Certain aspects of human nature, which we have socially suppressed, were dialled up, and other aspects were dialled down. Charting a course with characters that is true to the time but also accessible to a modern reader is a fun challenge. On the other hand, the generally received wisdom that the medieval era was only violent, filthy, disease ridden with a few bright sparks of art and literature, is patently not true. I enjoy challenging those preconceptions through my books.

What inspired you to write this particular story?

Richard II gets short shrift as a king. Some of that poor opinion is deserved, and some of it isn't. His ill-advised attempt to invade Scotland has garnered a lot of scorn without many of his detractors looking too closely at key factors such as his youth and inexperience, the weight of expectations – possibly unreasonable expectations, and the fact that his own lords were already quarrelling before the army was formed (everyone would much rather have been going to France – something many holiday makers can relate to no doubt – but no one really wanted to pay for it). In addition, several occurrences on the way seem to have further cast a pall on the occasion. It was the perfect rats' nest of difficulties to launch Gregory into with a mission most lords would baulk at.

If you were transported back to the time your story is set, who is the first person you would want to talk to and why?

That's a no brainer – Geoffrey Chaucer. What writer wouldn't want to speak to the godfather of the English language? Christine de Pizan comes in a close second.

If there was one event in the period you could witness (in perfect safety) what would it be?

So many things went catastrophically wrong for Richard II – big, reign shaping events too. From a historical interest standpoint, I'd want to watch the Merciless Parliament.

However, I think I'd most like to see Chaucer and Gower performing their various works. Reading in the fourteenth century was a social event because books were so scarce. If you had a book, you were supposed to be reading aloud to all present – a form of entertaining that ladies took part in. Reading alone was considered the height of bad manners and selfishness. (Something that Richard II was accused of since he often brought books to meals and read privately). Chaucer in particular wrote his poems to be read aloud not just at noble gatherings but in inns and taverns and marketplaces. The commoners were not ill-educated and illiterate – most could read, just not in Latin. Considering who his audience was, it's no surprise that Chaucer, who was quite the polyglot, wrote so much of his work in Middle English.

Why do you think readers are still so thirsty for stories from this period?

Historical fiction is the ultimate adventure holiday. You visit the past and live for a while under a different set of norms, values and social codes. You get to experience a life that is in some ways less complicated and in other ways veers far closer to danger and death. And then, most importantly, you are allowed to leave. I think medieval fiction appeals especially to those who want to experience battles, political intrigues and social customs which are very different from our own.

What are you writing at the moment?

I also write sci-fi and fantasy, so I'm working on a

separate project in that genre. Historical fiction wise, I'm writing a series set a few years after *Tyrant* which continues Gregory's adventures but also follows those of his grown up, younger son, Lionel.

How important is it for you to be part of a community of writers, and why?

Writing can be a very solitary endeavour so a group of peers and friends you can bounce ideas off and exchange tips with is essential. A good writing buddy can help you to keep going when you hit a sticky point, and who else could you discuss your characters and their motives with in obsessive detail?

Where can readers find out more about your books?

I post snippets on twitter and readers can follow me there @J_AnneIronside (fair warning, there will be pictures of jousting snails and penis trees – Medieval margin art is weird.) You can also find my books on Amazon, Fantastic Fiction and Goodreads. My main home on the internet is my webpage www.jaironside.com – where you can also sign up for my newsletter and find various bits of news, deals and freebies. I love hearing from fans! You can contact me by email at jaironsideauthor@gmail.com

A Plague on Your Business by Michael Jecks

The body was wrapped at last. He had carefully washed her, combing her hair and covering it with a clean linen coif, gently setting her arms at her sides, wiping away his own tears as he worked.

Berenger Fripper had not laid out a body in an age. This was work for women - but in this time of pestilence, all stayed away from corpses. Those who had been touched by the evil buboes must die alone and unshriven. No one wanted to go near in case they might also find themselves afflicted. Some said it was a sign of God's disgust. Berenger knew that was wrong. God could not have wanted to punish his Marguerite. He deserved His justice more. Perhaps this was a punishment for his wrongs?

He picked up the little bundle and placed it carefully on her breast, crossing her arms about it, pressing it tight against her breast.

"There, my love, there. You protect him when you face God together. Keep him with you and … and -"

He could manage no more. Breaking down, he knelt at the side of the table, his brow resting on his dead wife's flank, his hand still on his son's tiny figure, as the hot, angry tears flowed and the sobs threatened to choke him. He was alone again. Never before had he felt such desperate solitude. As a professional soldier, he had enjoyed the comfort and companionship of other men about him, laughing and joking through the good times and the ill but now, since he had taken the offer of a house here in Calais after Edward III had won the city, he was without friends. Old Jacob had died earlier in the week, and his neighbour Fletcher was even now in the last stages of his disease. All those whom he had called friends, he had waved off as they sailed homewards, their purses filled with French gold. Sir John de Sully, Grandarse and his archers, all gone. Not that they would be any safer in England from this disease. Nowhere was safe. God had deserted His people. God was destroying all.

There was a knock and a muffled shout. Berenger wiped his eyes and snorted hard to clear his nose, then made his way out through the little shop to the front door. He opened it to be confronted by a man who stood a wary pace or two away.

'Where?' the man asked. He had a cloth tied about his nose and mouth. It did not prevent the reek of strong wine reaching Berenger's nose. He didn't grudge the man a drink. His was not a job many would wish to take.

Berenger led the way to the parlour where the two lay on his table. He felt another sob from deep in his belly rise up as though to throttle him. It lodged in his throat like a rock, and he could not speak.

The man entered and gazed down at the bodies. 'Your child as well?'

Berenger nodded.

'Godspeed them both, friend,' the collector said and crossed himself.

Berenger busied himself covering her face, once so beautiful, now so empty of feeling and emotion. With the thick needle and waxed twine, he stitched from her feet in great loops that caught the shroud and bunched it up like badly knitted scars. He had to take more twine when he reached her breast, clumsily trying to thread the needle with hands that shook.

'Here, let me,' the carter said, but Berenger snatched his hands away before the man could grab them.

'No!'

This was his wife, and he would see to her remains as best he could. He didn't need another man's help, another man's hands pawing at her.

'Hurry up, eh?' the man said gruffly. He pulled the cloth aside and scratched at his chin before pulling the mask back.

Berenger clenched his jaw, and the thread slipped through the eye. He took up a handful of the shroud and began to stitch. He wouldn't have a stranger getting so close to his Marguerite's breast. It was hateful that the man could see her like this without setting his hands near her. He paused as the needle reached her chin. While he could see her face, he almost felt the life might return to her. Covering her face was the final act. Once hidden, she would be gone forever. He lingered, staring at her, clenching his jaw, willing her to move, to open her eyes, to smile at him ...

But she would not. He steeled himself, and covered her face, stitching quickly as a fresh inundation of tears flooded his cheeks. It was done. She was gone.

The two carried the bundle out to the road to the waiting cart. There were already three bodies lying there: the morning's haul from only a pair of streets. Before the carter reached the end of this roadway, the cart would be full. The wailing and sobbing from all over the city bore testament to the misery of all as carts like this took away their loved ones.

Berenger climbed onto the cart's bed and took his wife and child from the carter, He laid the little parcel down with care, moving another figure to give his wife and child a little more space. Then he clambered down leadenly, and stared as the cart began to clatter off over the cobbles, the figures in the back jerking with every rut and stone as the wheels rattled on.

He was empty. There was nothing in him but a great void. He wanted nothing now; only the oblivion that wine would bring. But he was rooted to the spot, blind to everything but this last glimpse of his wife and child. He watched as the carter stopped a few doors farther along the street, knocking at the timbers, standing aside as two servants brought out the heavy body of Berenger's near-neighbour, Master Richard. The corpulent figure was slumped between them like a sack of turnips and the carter was forced to help them, grabbing the feet while the servants held tight to the shoulders. The men struggled, the carter hauling while the two servants attempted to push the figure up, and Berenger saw the carter stand on his wife's corpse.

He bellowed, and a sudden rage overwhelmed him at the sight of his Marguerite being trampled. His scalp tightened, and he had a clenching in his belly as though a fist was gripping his stomach, and he started to run at the cart. The carter had the winding sheet now, and gripped the dead man's body under the armpits, tugging. One of the servants joined him on the cart, and the two succeeded in lifting the body to sit on the edge. Some of the winding sheet snagged on a splinter or a nail, and the servant below tugged to free it.

It was then that the carter saw Berenger running at him. He cried out to the servants in alarm, before yanking hard at the body. There was a ripping as the corpse's covering tore, and while the servant and carter pushed and shoved, the sheet came away, and Berenger saw the wide-eyed face, the pale features, the loosely moving arms of his neighbour.

The carter turned, knelt on the board and snapped the reins. The horse jerked, began to move while the servant sprang down, and before Bringer could reach the masked carter, he had rumbled his way round the corner.

Berenger ran on a few paces, fuelled by the anger that roiled in his breast, and then, suddenly, he stopped, and almost dropped to the ground as the bitter misery gripped him like an ague.

One of the servants recognised him and stood uncertainly while Berenger covered his face with his hands, trying to get a grip on himself. All he could see was the body of his Marguerite and baby being trampled by the carter.

'Master?'

Berenger glanced at the closed features, the weary, peevish expression of a man impatient with expressions of grief. Everyone had suffered, everyone had lost. What right did Berenger have to indulge himself?

'Leave me!' Berenger snapped, feeling the rage grow. He ran, and when he turned the corner, he saw the cart half-way up the next road. There was a woman in the street, weeping, and the carter had pulled up, dropping from the step like a man sapped of all energy.

In the back of the cart, Berenger saw his neighbour's body resting on top of his wife's. The breath stopped in his breast for a moment, and then he gave an inarticulate bellow and ran straight for the carter. He had no thoughts of his actions, only a blind, unreasoning hatred: for the carter, for the city, for the land which had once seemed so full of promise, and now was filled only with death and destruction. It was as if he was swimming in a sea of blood. All about him was red, raw with rage and hatred.

He didn't even know he was hitting the man until he was pulled away. Panting, struggling to free himself, he stared wide-eyed as the carter was helped up from the ground. He was shaking his head like a dog drying after a dip in a river, blood running from his nose.

'Let him loose,' he said. 'It wasn't his fault. He's lost his family.'

Berenger's arms were released, and he clenched his fists, but only to press them to his eyes as he fought to keep the tears at bay. He had nothing inside him, no more anger. Just this all-consuming emptiness. 'I saw … you stood on them,' he said brokenly, staring at the corpses in the back of the cart. His Marguerite was still concealed in her winding sheet, but next to her was the merchant. His cold, dead eyes like those of a fish on a slab.

'I lost my mind,' Berenger said. It felt as though a leather strap had been placed about his head, and was tightening as he spoke. Fleeting glimpses of Marguerite kept flashing into his mind; pictures of her laughing, smiling, feeding their son …

'That man hasn't died from the plague,' one man said.

Berenger glanced at him, then back to the dead Richard.

'There are none of the marks of the plague, no buboes, no stench... he isn't stiff.'

'It takes time for a body to stiffen,' said the carter.

'He died a while ago. Look at him!'

They all knew. They had seen enough corpses, especially in the last couple of years while the English armies ranged over France, and now, with the corpses piling daily.

A man and woman were watching, and Berenger overheard them.

'<u>She</u> won't miss him, you mark my words. Never was there a more brazen hussy. She'll be entertaining her menfolk with pleasure, now that they can visit without risking her cuckold husband's displeasure,' the woman said, short and plump like a hen.

The man was milder. 'Come now, mistress! You cannot seriously believe that! Mistress Alice has lost her husband.'

'I'll bet her purse won't be any the lighter,' the woman said tartly. 'With all her <u>admirers</u> she won't go without!'

'Admirers!' the man scoffed.

'As if you would know! Who would blame her? Master Richard couldn't keep his tarse in his hosen. She told him loud enough for the street to hear that he must throw over his latest wench only last week.'

Berenger rounded on her. He knew the woman. 'You would accuse her, Gossip, when her husband is barely cold? You spread malice for no reason other than to bolster your own self-importance,' Berenger snapped. She gasped, and the man with her opened his mouth to remonstrate, but Berenger had heard enough. He turned on his heel and made his way homewards.

It was late in the afternoon that the knock came at his door. Berenger's maidservant had left when Marguerite first began to show symptoms of the disease raging through her body, and he must shift for himself. After years of marching with the King's armies, he was competent to make oatcakes and cook pottage or roast a rabbit, so he did not miss a cook, but he grunted with annoyance when the rap on the timbers came a second time.

'Well?'

Outside stood the carter, unhappily screwing his cap in his hands. Behind him was a man of middle-height, with the broad shoulders and thick neck of a man used to fighting. He stood with his head lowered truculently. 'Berenger Fripper?'

'What of it?'

'I am John of Furnshill, of Sir John de Sully's retinue. I would be grateful for a talk.'

Berenger eyed him for a moment before nodding. Soon they were sitting before his fire.

It was John who spoke. 'You know of the death of your neighbour, Master Richard Allchard?'

'Yes,' Berenger said, giving a cold glance at the carter.

'There have been rumours suggesting that his widow could have been responsible for his death. Do you think that?'

'How should I know? I am a dealer in clothing, not a Keeper of the King's Peace!'

'But you do know her?'

'I have met her.'

'And you were happy enough to defend her name.'

Berenger groaned inwardly. His temper had got the better of him and now it had got him into trouble. 'I heard a woman maligning her, and -'

'And you defended her. There must be a reason for that. You were a soldier once, so I doubt it was a merely altruism on your part.'

'My wife has died. I just … I didn't want to see Mistress Allchard pilloried for something when she's grieving for her husband.'

'Others feel the same,' John said. He stared at Berenger. His eyes were a very dark colour, and under that intense gaze, Berenger grew increasingly uncomfortable. It made him grow choleric, but before he could blurt out an angry remark, the fellow jerked his head toward at the carter. 'You saw the body. This man reported it.'

The carter threw a plaintive look at Berenger.

'He had no buboes, and he was coming out of rigor mortis,' John said flatly. 'He did not die of the plague.'

'Perhaps he just didn't show the same symptoms.'

'He had none. He died a little while before, long enough for the rigor to wear off, and then his household kept his body until the carter was coming down the road already. Others say he was murdered. People suspect his widow guilty guilty. They clamour for her head.'

'Perhaps she did it.'

'Perhaps she did. But Sir John de Sully would not willingly see her pay for another's criminal act. He asked that you should conduct enquiries.'

'Me? Why me?'

John of Furnshill gave a twisted grin. 'Perhaps Sir John feels you still owe him service?'

***

Berenger rapped on the door with his knuckles and stood back. Everyone tried to keep away from others in case the pestilence might migrate from one to another, but Berenger was careless of danger. His wife was dead. Death held no fear for him.

A servant with eyes rather close-set and a thin face opened the door.

'Tell your mistress I would speak with her.'

After a brief delay while the man explained she was in mourning and not seeing visitors, Berenger pushed his foot against the door and shoved it wide. The man squeaked and placed his hand on his dagger, but Berenger quickly grasped his hand and forced it away. An archer's grip is second only to a blacksmith's, and the servant paled as his fingers were crushed like so many pea-pods.

A voice called to him before Berenger could quite break them. 'Master Fripper, I would be glad if you didn't damage my staff.'

Berenger turned, releasing the man, who gave a whimper and clutched his hand to his breast.

She stood in the screens passage, pale and resolute. Waving away her servant, she motioned towards a parlour, and Berenger followed her inside.

Mistress Alice was no beauty. Her face was too round, her eyes too wide-spaced, her mouth too thin, but for all that, there was a vivacity about her that was appealing. Berenger could easily imagine that she would ensnare a lover. Not that she was showing signs of such appeal just now. Her eyes were red-rimmed, as were her nostrils. She had tried to keep her hair beneath her coif, but bedraggled strands dangled. When she tried to smile, she looked like a condemned woman pleading with her hangman.

'Well? What was so important you had to break my servant to speak to me of it?'

'Mistress, it gives me no pleasure to be here.'

'Why are you? Is it to accuse me? You wish to say that everyone thinks I killed poor Richard? That he was murdered by me? I know what the gossips say!'

To Berenger's consternation, she began to weep, her shoulders jerking, although she made no sound.

'Mistress, I am sorry,' he said.

'Everyone is sorry, yet they accuse me. Well, I have not killed anyone, and certainly not my husband. Yes, he took many mistresses, but he always has. Why should I kill him?'

'Perhaps he died of natural causes?' Berenger guessed.

'How can I tell? He began to complain of torment in his bowels, and then writhed on the floor. Nothing we did could help him.'

'His physician …?'

'Master Ashton? You think that sour-faced blood-taker would come to a house hearing someone was unwell, now that the pestilence is here? He refused to visit.'

Berenger had heard of Ashton, a physician who had served in Edward's armies, but whose knowledge was restricted to the mending of bones or phlebotomy. It was not surprising that he would avoid a house with the pestilence. 'Did you explain your husband was suffering?'

'Yes, but he would not come. Richard died and I sat up with him. We called the Coroner, but he said he had no time. No one would come,' she said, and the tears ran without pause.

'Why would people say you killed him?'

'They are jealous? How should I know?'

'Do you have a lover?'

'How can you ask me a question like that?' she spat, but did not deny it.

'Who is he? Others will tell me if you don't,' he said.

She tried to refuse but finally threw up her hands in resentful submission. 'Andrew Peachi, if you must know!'

Berenger had little desire to question Peachi. He had met the man: a vain, fool of some five-and-thirty years. The idea of renewing his acquaintance was not appealing. 'Your husband had no sign of the plague?'

'No.'

'And there was no mark on his flesh? I assume you did search his body?'

'I looked, and so did my steward, but there was no wound.'

'So it must have been something he ate,' Berenger said. 'If there was murder done here, the only means must have been poison. What did he eat that evening?'

'He and I ate the same foods,' she said.

'Which were?'

'We had some Norwegian pasties, meat brewet, a roast of beef, a larded broth, a blankmanger, fresh fruits, and ... oh, I can't remember. Speak to the cook.'

***

The cook was a lugubrious, scrawny fellow, like a man who did not enjoy his own food. He was stirring a heavy pottage when Berenger entered the kitchen, and lambasting the kitchen boy for spilling a quantity of gravy.

Seeing Berenger, the cook snarled, 'Get out of my kitchen! I have a meal to prepare, and only a little time to do it!'

'I am here to learn what happened to your master, Cook, and if you don't want it cut from your mouth, you'll keep a civil tongue.'

The man gaped, unused to being threatened in his own place of work, but as Berenger stood and gazed at him truculently, the aggression dribbled away like thin soup through a sieve. He told the kitchen boy to keep stirring his pot and walked to a stool by the table. He poured a cup of weak wine and sipped. 'My apologies, Master, I didn't realise. I'm only a poor cook, when all is said and done. How can I help you?'

'Your master died after eating your food.'

'That wasn't my fault!'

'I am trying to find out what killed him. It may have been an accident. 'What did he eat that evening?'

It appeared that the merchant had eaten well that evening, it being not a fish day. There were pasties with beef and marrow, Norwegian pasties with cod's livers, a white coney brewet, a roast, a blankmanger … Berenger felt his mind whirl at the list. 'Was there anything that he ate that his wife did not?'

'No. The Norwegian pasties were for Mistress, but they ate everything else.'

'Why were they only for her?'

'She likes them,' he shrugged. 'Master had never eaten them before, so I made them.'

'How did you like your master?'

'Well. He was a good man,' the fellow said. He aimed a kick at the kitchen boy. 'Stir that pottage!'

'What of the rest of the house? Did all think him a good master?'

'Yes. This was a happy house. Although …'

'What?'

The Cook twisted his head in the manner of a man talking of a woman, as though implying carnal knowledge. It was enough to make Berenger want to punch him. He clenched his fist, but kept it at his side. 'Well?' he demanded.

'She has a friend, a man called Peachi,' the Cook said, nodding knowledgeably.

'What do you know of him?'

'Little enough. I am sure he is a pleasant enough fellow,' the Cook leered. He gave a short sound like a snigger. Berenger stepped forward, and would have punched him, but as he moved, there was a loud crash, and then a scream. He whirled about and ran along the passageway, out to the front door.

In the road there was a woman, perhaps mid-twenties, hurling abuse at the house. On seeing Berenger, she picked up a stone from the road and flung it with all her strength at him. He ducked aside and it struck the door-frame and rattled along the flags of the screens passage, Berenger glanced at the house, and saw that she had thrown other stones. One had flown through the window of the hall, and he had no doubt the stone had struck a pot or bowls to make the noise he had heard.

'You killed him, you cow! You foul old hag! You murdered my man, didn't you? Just because you couldn't bear to share him, you decided to tear his heart from him! You ended his life as surely as if you'd used a sword or a dagger!'

There was much more in a similar vein, and she didn't resist when Berenger took her hand and wrested a fresh stone from her grip. 'Come, maid. Where do you live? You cannot stand in the roadway here.'

'Why not? She his murdered him! She must have done!' the woman said, and then her head fell into her hands and she began to sob.

***

He took her to the little tavern at the top of the road. Berenger had visited this place many times with his wife, and it held fond memories. The tavernkeeper, John Barrow, was a great bull of a man, with a moustache that swept back to his ears and a constantly dark jaw where the beard threatened within a half hour of the barber's visit. He had shoulders like a wrestler, and his arms were as thick as young oaks. But now he was diminished. Two months ago he had been the father of four children. Now he had lost all and was widowed. He sat in the corner of the tavern and gazed blearily at Berenger. Berenger served himself from a small barrel of red wine. Dropping coins on the counter, he picked up two cups which he took it back to the table where the girl was waiting. Setting the cups before her, he poured from the jug and sat.

'Who are you?' he asked.

'I am Marianne Ashton.'

'Daughter of the physician?'

'What of it?'

'Nothing. I was merely wondering that you began your affair with a man who must have been one of your father's wealthiest clients.'

'He was a kind, good man. I loved poor Richard. Gracious God! I loved him so!'

'How did you meet him?'

'At my father's chamber, paying for his last blood-letting. He was often around when I was at home.'

Berenger could imagine why. Marianne had bright eyes of a greenish colour, and her skin was faultless, smooth and unblemished, with pink flaring at her cheeks. Her neck was as slender as a swan's, her face regular, the mouth full and apparently prone to smiling, from the light creases at either side. She was a lovely woman, and it was all too easy to see that a man like Richard, who Berenger knew had a roving eye, would be entranced.

'But you knew he was married.'

She sniffed, and gulped wine, refilling her cup. 'Of course I knew. But it was a dead marriage. They wed for advantage, but he wanted me for love,' she added, eyes watering. 'She poisoned him. She killed him. She must pay for her treason.'

'Why would she kill him? Was he cruel? Did he beat her?'

'Richard would not have beaten a rabid dog! No, she killed him because she is jealous! She could not bear to think that he might be happy with another. She could not tolerate his choosing someone other than her.'

***

Berenger walked her back to her house.

Before they left, Berenger set the remaining wine in the jug before the tavern-keeper. The man looked grateful, but it was hard to tell. Berenger thought he might return and help the man drink the remaining wine in his cellar. Why not? He craved the oblivion of strong wine.

Her home was the apothecary's shop, a sign declaring that the master here was used to dealing with the English. Any tradesman had to declare that, since the siege and the capture of the town by King Edward III. Berenger rapped on the timbers of the door.

The man who opened it was tall and lugubrious, with mournful eyes. He looked from Berenger to Marianne and back, and he seemed to shrivel at the sight. 'Who are you? What do you want?'

'My name is Berenger Fripper, and I brought her home before she could be arrested for lobbing stones at another woman's house.'

'Oh, Marianne, what now?' the man groaned.

'She killed him, father. You know that as well as I.'

'I know nothing of the sort. Friend, Master Fripper, I am glad you brought her home. You have my gratitude. And now …' he turned, beckoning his daughter in to join him.

'One moment, Physician. Why did you not go when Mistress Alice called you? She said her husband was unwell, but you did not go to him.'

'I was engaged with another client. I could not go. Have you not noticed that the pestilence is all about you? It is here in the air. Every breath you take out of doors will see you succumb the sooner, especially at night when it is most virulent. I could not think of going to him then. And I was with another client.'

'Which client?'

'That is none of your business,' the man said. He held Berenger's gaze as he slowly pulled the door closed.

The sound of bolts sliding home came to Berenger. 'You, master, are lying,' he murmured.

***

Andrew Peachi was a slim, elegant man in his middle thirties, a man nearer to Alice's age than her husband had been. Peachi was round-faced, but with a lively sparkle in his eyes that spoke of his adventurous nature.

He smiled when Berenger entered his house. 'Master Fripper, I think? We have met before.'

'Yes, Master Peachi. At the house of Sir John de Sully. You were there with a fresh conquest.'

'Conquest?'

'I've known many men treat women as toys to be played with and then discarded. Beatrice of Sens was infatuated with you until her death. Was it because of you she died?'

Peachi's smile fell away and he grew sorrowful. 'That was a terrible thing. They say that she slipped while she was walking along the quayside.'

'They often say such things to save the poor and afflicted from being accused of self-murder,' Berenger said.

His words unsettled Peachi. 'Some women cannot accept that they have become superseded. I fear that Beatrice was sweet, very sweet, but not very mature. She was little better than a child.'

'You took advantage of her and that led to her self-killing.'

'Oh, really!' he waved a hand airily. 'She couldn't understand when our relationship was over. It was clear enough that there was no more for us. She wanted to continue, but, what could I say? It was too late.'

'Because you had another woman lined up: Alice.'

'I wouldn't -'

'She has already told me that she was having an affair with you,' Berenger said.

A smile crossed Peachi's face. Another conquest; another addition to his reputation.

Berenger nodded. 'So you had a desire to see her husband removed.'

The smile fled from his face like quicksilver from a tilted bowl. 'You cannot mean that.'

'You wanted her; you wanted the freedom to take her whenever you wanted; you wanted the risk of her husband removed. It must have been galling, taking on a married woman - not a young wench you could easily pursue, but a woman who was unfree and married. You must have seen her as a more inspiring challenge - but then - what? You decided you wanted her entirely for yourself? You could not bear to share her with another? A situation easily resolved with poison in her husband's food. Much safer than stabbing him in the street, much safer than risking yourself. Did you bribe the cook?'

Peachi's shook his head. 'Challenge? Yes, she was a challenge, but less difficult than she might have been. Richard's womanising was flagrant, and he rubbed her face in his conquests all too often. She was a willing partner, for a while. But she still loved him. She told me it was over. You think I killed him? I know nothing about poisons, and I know no one in the house apart from her! If someone killed her husband, it must have been she herself!'

'I will be sure to tell her that is what you believe.'

'Do so! You think I'd live with a woman who could murder her own husband?' the man sneered.

Berenger rose. 'So you will not support her now?'

'You think me a fool? Everyone would be sure to comment on my relationship with her!'

Berenger nodded, and then his fist lashed out. He caught Peachi below the rib-cage, and the fellow bent almost double as the air whooshed from him, and then Berenger hit the side of his head and the man collapsed. A kick to his cods left him gasping, clutching at his damaged privates, rolling on the stone floor.

'If I hear you've tried to pin cuckold's horns on another man, I will castrate you,' he said, and left the room.

***

He returned to the tavern. John Barrow was still in his corner, but now there were three jugs on the floor about him, and he was weeping inconsolably. Berenger poured him more wine and sat beside him with his own cup. It was growing dark outside, and in a few moments John passed out, his head against the wall, his mouth wide, snoring a rasping, dirge-like tune that rose and fell, rose and fell.

Berenger drank cup after cup, but his mind would not rest. He saw his wife and child: Marianne smiling and happy, laughing; naked in the candle light that brought a golden glow to her body; in the river, her sleeves rolled up as she beat the clothes clean in the river's water; cooking, pushing the hair from her face as she perspired over the oven or brew pots ... then pale and dead as he sewed the last stitches in her winding sheet.

Suddenly something struck him: a cook making little pasties ... if they had been made for Allchard, it would have been easy to see who was guilty of the murder. But these were Alice Allchard's favourite ...

He stood and shivered. Leaving the tavern, he walked homewards and fell into his bed. Waking in the middle of the night, he threw his hand out, but it encountered only cold sheets. He sobbed then, until sleep took him once more. Never had he felt so alone.

***

The next morning, he woke, thrust his head into the trough before his house, and made his way back to the widow's house.

Alice was seated in her hall when he entered. 'Mistress, your chef told me that he made pasties for you because your husband didn't like them.'

'He did? He made the pasties because he knows they are my favourite dainties, but I had none. My husband had never tried them, but he found they were to his taste, and ate them all. I was happy he enjoyed them.'

Berenger nodded slowly. The cook had made the pasties for her, and her husband had eaten them. Were they poisoned? The idea that had formed in his mind the previous night came back in full force. He asked for the cook to be brought to him.

The man was pale and sweat glistened on his brow. 'Well?'

'Who told you to make those pasties?'

The man shiftily glanced at his mistress. 'I -'

'Look at me! Who suggested them?'

'The master.'

'He had not tried them. You said they were dainties for Mistress Alice.'

'They were! He knew she loved them!'

'Yet he ate them all.'

'I … He must have discovered he liked them too.'

'A man who asks for a treat for his wife would hardly be so crass as to eat it himself and deprive her. Who told you to make them?'

'My sister!'

'Your sister?'

'Yes.'

***

It took little effort to have him confess after that, and soon Berenger was outside the physician's house with John of Furnshill.

'I hope you are correct, Master Fripper.'

'If you don't trust my judgement, go and tell Sir John that I have failed,' Berenger snapped and knocked.

There was a brief interval while both men stood waiting. When the door opened, Berenger was shocked to see the pale, drawn expression on the face of the maid. 'What has happened?'

'The poor little chit! The poor thing!' the maid said.

They found Ashton in his parlour, cradling his daughter's body. He looked up with raw eyes that flamed at the sight of Berenger. 'This is your doing!'

'What has happened?' John of Furnshill demanded.

'She was distraught at poor Master Allchard's death. So distressed …'

'No,' Berenger said. He walked to the table and sat.

'Why? What do you say?'

'This: your daughter planned to kill Mistress Alice. She learned of a tempting dainty that Alice would eat, and persuaded her brother, your son and the Allchards' cook, to add something. I doubt he knew what it was, but afterwards he realised. As you did. Was it something missing from your stores? She took poison and your son unwittingly killed his master. Because his master suddenly learned that he liked this new dainty, and his wife, enjoying his pleasure, willingly allowed him to finish it. That was why your daughter yesterday accused Alice of murder, because Alice should have eaten them all herself. Instead, Marianne discovered that her plan had killed her lover. As you knew. That was why you chose not to visit the house to see Richard's death throes.'

'I guessed. How could I have guessed? It never occurred to me that Marianne could have thought to do such a thing. And it was her lover whom she killed, not her rival. And now I have lost her!'

'She is little loss to you,' John said flatly as he stood again. 'But justice has been served.'

'Surely there is no need to tell anyone? She died in her sleep, and it was an accident.'

Berenger answered: 'She took her own life from despair after realising she had slain her lover. If her guilt is concealed, Alice will suffer. She is the only innocent in this sad affair. So no, Marianne's guilt will not be concealed, nor will her self-murder.'

'You would threaten her soul? She is dead, Master Fripper! Show mercy!'

'I give you respect for your loss, but mercy for her? She murdered a man, meaning to kill another from jealousy and greed. My concern lies with the living.'

***

They walked out a little later, the pair of them silent. In the street they saw another collector's cart laden with the dead, and the two averted their faces as it passed.

'I am grateful to you for your help,' John of Furnshill said.

'It is nothing.'

'What will you do now?'

Berenger considered the question. He thought of his house, now so empty; of Alice and her husband; of Marianne and her brother; and finally of the tavern - but he said nothing.

'Why did Sir John de Sully ask me to investigate?'

'Why do you think?'

'I can only think because he wanted Alice to be free of suspicion. Perhaps he knew her husband? Or, perhaps he knew her and did not want her to be maligned?'

'Sir John is not young. When he was a youth, he met a woman, and had a daughter. I doubt many men would wish to see their children accused of murder.'

Interview with Michael Jecks

Can you tell us a bit about yourself? How long have you been writing and what other jobs have you had?

I have been writing for some twenty-six year now. I was originally a computer salesman working in office automation, but after a run of thirteen jobs in thirteen years, I decided it was time to take the hint, and started writing in 1994. THE LAST TEMPLAR was accepted that year by Headline, and I felt my future was at least a little more secure than it had been selling computers!

What is it about the Medieval Period that inspires you?

Initially it was the thought of chivalry and knights in armour riding off on quests, but as a youngster I started to spend more time researching their codes and actions, and soon learned that they were not always honourable or even chivalrous. Which was why I began to get interested in the case of the Knights Templar and the atrocious treatment meted out to them.

What inspired you to write this particular story?

My Vintener Trilogy was rather a passion of mine. It covers Crécy in FIELDS OF GLORY, and then BLOOD ON THE SAND was about the siege of Calais. The three books were always intended to look at the lives of a small band of archers, and their experiences in those two battles, and then the final conflict that led to Poitiers. But Poitiers happened after the Black Death, and I always wanted to look at that too from the perspective of one of them. This book gave me the opportunity!

What do you enjoy most about writing?

For me, it is the contemplation. I love getting inside the heads of other people and imagining their lives, their problems, their worlds. For me it is almost a form of recreation to be able to set aside my own troubles and think about other people. To be able to look at people and how they used to live is a wonderful way to earn a living.

If you were transported back to the time your story is set, who is the first person you would want to talk to and why?

A small village's priest. I have less interest in the lives of kings and princes, but to have a chance to talk to a religious man of the time would mean learning about the importance of the seasons, of superstition, of the lives of all the local people - that would be wonderful.

If there was one event in the period you could witness (in perfect safety) what would it be?

The meeting between Edward II and the delegation sent to him to demand his abdication in favour of his son. It would be fascinating to see Edward's reaction - a man convinced about his own position in the world, certain of God's support for him and the Throne, who saw it all topple about him.

Why do you think readers are still so thirsty for stories from this period?

How could they not be? This was the beginning of the modern age, when concepts of democracy, government and humanitarianism were all being developed and evolving. In addition, it harks back to an age when life was a great deal more simple. People were more concerned with whether they would have enough food to fill the bellies of their children, rather than whether they should buy the latest mobile phone or gaming device. There is an attraction to such simplicity, when viewed from the position of relative wealth and comfort that we enjoy today.

What are you writing at the moment?

Just now I am writing a novel based on the reign of Bloody Mary Tudor. I've been writing about Jack Blackjack for six years now. He's an engaging rogue, an incompetent pickpocket and thief, who happens to have been given a job that is completely beyond him: that of assassin. But it pays well, and means he has been given a house and wardrobe of the latest fashions, so he reckons he can keep the benefits until his inability to murder people at his master's request is spotted. The books are light-hearted, as you may have gathered, and I enjoy writing them immensely, throwing the poor devil into as many dangerous scrapes as possible and seeing how he manages to survive!

How important is it for you to be part of a community of writers, and why?

Writing is a very solitary occupation, and I think very few authors would be able to cope without the support of a strong group of friends. Personally, I have been fortunate enough to call many authors in my area friends, and have regularly met with ten to fifteen historical and crime writers for lunches. For people in other professions, there is a very important camaraderie built upon shared experience, shared interests and the daily grind. Authors do not have that. There is no coffee machine where authors congregate daily. To have occasional email conversations about publishers and editors is an important release that saves a lot of mental anguish!

Where can readers find out more about your books?

The best resource for information on me and my books is my website at www.michaeljecks.co.uk. There I have a complete list of all of my books from the Templar Series, the Vintener Trilogy, the Crusades titles and modern thrillers, all in the order in which the books were written. There is also a newsletter where interested people can receive regular updates about my writing and future events.

A Matter of Honour by Peter Sandham

'It's a matter of honour,' said the condotierro captain, Baldo Maruffo, to the best man of his mercenary company.

John Grant's young face contorted with perplexity as it did sometimes when he heard a new Genoese phrase for the first time. 'Honour? I thought that was something we couldn't afford. "Honour's too dear. Let dukes and kings have honour, we'll settle for bread and being alive." Isn't that your motto?'

Maruffo guided the Scotsman to the edge of the bustling road.

'Well today's a little different, John.'

'Aye, it's carnival Sunday,' replied Grant, 'and for once we are not spending it on a Lombardy battlefield.' He gestured to the buildings surrounding them: the tall, stone houses with painted shutters; the towers and compound walls built to shield one banking family from another; the top-heavy bridge spanning the river, crowded with butchers. It was the Scotsman's first visit to Florence. The reaction was always the same.

'I'm not planning on being honourable tonight, Baldo,' Grant added. 'Florence has too many pretty ladies for that sentiment.'

'Naturally, you think like that: you're young and single minded. But if we were on that Lombardy field, we'd be earning a crust. Florence and its pretty ladies are fun. They are also expensive. The company needs a contract.'

'I understand that.'

'Which requires impressing the right people.'

'Certainly.'

'Well today the Good Lord is presenting us with a fine chance to do just that. Have you ever heard of Constantinople, John?'

'Course I have, Baldo! Christ's balls, do you think I was raised by bloody wolves!'

'I sometimes wonder lad. Hey - a joke - no need to pout. Point is, the Greek Emperor and half his court have been in Italy this past year, talking themselves silly at Ferrara about things which don't concern us. The plague decided to join them there, so the whole talking shop has uprooted and moved to Florence. Emperor and all. They arrived yesterday and, of course, Cosimo de Medici is keen to put on a glorious show.'

The pair reached the wide Piazza della Signoria and Grant saw that it had been transformed. The redbrick palazzo still loomed on one side with its single, thin tower rising like a rebuking finger, but the centre of the square had vanished overnight beneath a circular mountain of tiered wooden benches.

Grant stopped in his tracks. 'An arena? They're not going to force the Emperor to watch Florentine football, are they?'

'Fortunately not,' said Maruffo. 'This stadium is for something that will allow you to showcase our military talents better than a calcio match.'

'Hell, Baldo! I should have known. A bloody Roman Emperor in town, of course that mad banker Cosimo would revive the colosseum. Honour? Pah! Just hand me the trident and net and tell me which poor man I'm to kill.'

'John, please, this is Italy, not your barbaric island. The

Emperor is a pious lover of philosophy. Even Cosimo might be a back-alley cutpurse at heart, but he knows how to hide it under silk manners. Their tastes are refined and heroic. They want Theseus not Spartacus. You're going to fight a bull.'

'Mother of Christ!'

'There's also more than just an Emperor watching the festivities. The Duke of Milan has an agent here looking to hire troops for the summer campaign. I've been told our company is on a shortlist of two. The other is Francesco Sforza's mercenaries, so you had better outdo Sforza's man in the arena or that fat contract will go his way and not ours. A matter of honour, as I said.'

'Sounds more like a matter of ducats.'

Maruffo shrugged. 'These days it amounts to the same thing. Come, let's get you ready.'

Maruffo explained that five condotierro companies in total had been invited to pit a man that afternoon against a bull in single combat. Those chosen would eschew the protection of armour, since there was no chivalry in a contest if a degree of mortal danger was not shared with an opponent. Instead they would dress only in pourpoint and leave their heads bare of cap or helm.

Keen-eyed for fashion, Maruffo chose for Grant a padded doublet, dyed an expensive black and studded like a star-field in tiny cowrie shells. He could not be missed by the Milanese agent.

'You'll look like the Duke of Burgundy by the time we are done lad,' Maruffo said proudly as he dragged Grant to a barber.

The blond highlander hair was neatly trimmed down and

146

Grant's beard, jutting off his chin like the ram of a trireme, oiled to a point. If he did not win them a contract that day, Grant reassured himself that he would doubtless win a few female hearts in the crowd.

Florence glowed in the afternoon winter sun, a terracotta Turkish carpet stitched by the silver thread of the Arno and spread among the gently rolling Tuscan hills. The main streets had been cleared by the Medici soldiers, forcing the people to clamber on rooftops or lean from windows to catch a glimpse of the procession. Under this aerial scrutiny, the line of Greek churchmen, lords and philosophers made the short walk from their lodgings at the Palazzo Peruzzi for the day's entertainment.

The displaced Byzantine court, which had come to beg deliverance from the growing Turkish menace with little to sell but the integrity of their faith, had taken their seats on the cushioned benches. Some were happier than others at the prospect of an afternoon's respite from religious debating. After more than a year of fruitless negotiation with Latins, some even felt deep empathy for the condemned bulls in the holding pen. The eyes of those animals betrayed an understanding of the ordeal ahead: the impossibility of escaping death; the sole remaining hope of making a good one.

A trumpet blew and the crowded benches of onlookers craned their necks to watch two mounted men canter across the ring to the raised platform containing the guests of honour. Doffing their hats, they received the Emperor's authority and galloped back to open the gate and allow in the procession of knights.

The five who would fight the bulls walked abreast, chins

raised and eyes on the standing figure of the Emperor. The men who would support their effort followed: grooms for the horses, the trusted sword and lance handlers and the mercenary captains whom each knight represented. They followed the hoof marks of the earlier riders and made their bow to the imperial box with the ritual air of a high mass.

Grant looked up and saw the gaunt face and large, sad eyes of the Emperor. A sickly pale man in his forties, he did not wear a smile of enthusiasm at the prospect before him. By contrast Cosimo de Medici sat on the Emperor's left with the look of a gambler for whom every card was turning up trumps. Only three years prior he had been imprisoned in the redbrick palazzo at his back. Now he practically owned Florence and had an Emperor as a houseguest.

Having made their bow, the formation of knights broke into little groups, each striding loose-hipped to a different part of the four-foot circular barricade of wood which protected the front row of benches from the killing floor.

It was only now, with the smell from the damp sand in his nostrils, that Grant's insides become restless serpents. He felt suddenly stupefied and clumsy and was gripped by a terrible fear that he would let Maruffo down in the moment.

For his own part, the Genoese mercenary captain showed no outward signs of concern. He passed a heavy gold brocaded cape to Grant and told him to drape it along the front wall.

Grant chose a spot that showed honour to the group of long-bearded Greek dignitaries sat there, but his choice stemmed more from the party of ladies eyeing him from three rows behind. He made a great show of smoothing the cape out and made the women blush with a wink.

While Grant set the cape on the barricade, the sand was raked clean of the procession's tracks. Those knights whose turn would come later retired with their entourage into the small gap between the first raised bench and the wooden parapet. Once Grant clambered over to join Maruffo, the only man left in the arena was Francesco Sforza's younger brother, Alessandro. He would fight the first bull.

The arena fell into silence and every eye turned to the red plank door through which the bull would be released. The Emperor had the honour of giving a signal with the drop of a red handkerchief. It fluttered down and splayed like a prophetic bloodstain on the sand.

The trumpet blew again. The bolt was slipped, and the door swung open.

The bull which emerged appeared confident and aggressive. Its pelt was glossy and thick, and its head made small by the pair of viciously sharp horns curving forward from it. Behind the short, thick neck, a sweating hump of muscle rose between wide shoulder blades. Its hooves were dainty, their light step belying the half-ton of muscle which they carried.

Like a rock from a catapult, it rushed across the arena toward the mounted man.

Alessandro Sforza waited with admirable serenity as the bull came at him, his back erect, his head held steady. Only the keenest-eyed horsemen in the crowd could detect the tension in his thighs and wrists, which was required to keep his mount under inch perfect control.

The bull was three strides into the charge when it occurred to Grant that Sforza was holding neither lance nor sword. 'My God, they've left him unarmed!'

'Fear not,' said Maruffo, watching intently beside him. 'He's not going to try and kill the thing on its first pass. He's sizing it up.'

Lowering its head, the bull came at the horse. Sforza took his mount out of danger in a nimble, cantering turn. For a beast of such size, the bull was agile as a spotted cat and able to turn much faster than Grant had expected.

'Mark that neck and those shoulders,' said Grant. 'It has the strength to lift and throw both horse and rider over its back.'

The bull, head lowered as if sniffing the hoofprints, followed Sforza's mount. Its horns were so close that each swish of the horsetail brushed their tips.

Round and round Sforza danced the horse. Round and round four times. Every tight turn forced the bull's spinal column to twist unnaturally and weary those matchstick limbs under their muscular burden. Gouts of breath came from the bull's widening nostrils and the gap between tail and horn widened until the bull came to a halt, its ferocity fully sapped from its legs.

With a wave to the rapturous crowd, Sforza cantered nonchalantly to the barrier and took a lance from his servant. Then, riding across the eye line of the beast, he goaded it into taking up the chase once more.

This time Sforza did not circle. Instead he led the bull straight across the arena. Grant studied how Sforza twisted around in the saddle to keep his eyes fixed on the bull. The horse - itself no fool - did something similar and so its carriage now was closer to a sideways prance than a gallop.

Had the bull the power of its first charge it would have bowled the horse over, but the circling had done its job. The tired bull could do little more than lollop, frustratingly close to its target, in a humiliating tour about the ring. Sforza waved to the crowd which showed suitably raucous appreciation for his clever, bold riding. Maruffo glanced anxiously towards the Milanese agent.

The bull concentrated its hatred on the horse and rider who had baffled him and taunted him and destroyed the confidence with which he had entered the ring. It put all its effort into closing the gap between the tips of its horns its target. The pair danced one last tour across the sand. The bull tossed its head upward, as if in hope its eyes deceived it and the horse was within range, but the horns found only air.

When its head dropped once more, Sforza struck.

All through the canter he kept the lance raised high, like a poised scorpion tail. It showed considerable strength: the blade on the lance was a foot long with four foot of ash shaft behind it. As the bull's head lowered and the humped muscle crest of its neck rippled upward, Sforza plunged the lance down.

In that moment, the horse prancing, the knight's arm thrusting the lance into the beast, it was a tableau worthy of Fra Angelico. The stroke had been delivered with precision, past the vertebrae and between the top of the ribs, slashing into the aorta. The bull was dead on its feet in the instant; its momentum bringing it crashing to the arena floor in a cloud of sand. By then Sforza's horse had nimbly side-stepped away.

It was a death which would have brought Julius Cesar to his feet in the colosseum. Instead, waving proudly from the saddle on a victorious lap of the ramshackle arena, Alessandro Sforza had to make do with John Palaiologos.

'Brave as a fighting cock,' Grant muttered. His eyes were fixed on the motionless body of the bull.

The next knight to fight was a local Florentine, but he proved an anti-climax for the home crowd. Less daring or less confident, he rode his horse around the arena edge and afforded the bull all the territory it desired. Unchallenged, the bull was content to paw the earth in the centre of the ring.

'They've given him a cowardly bull,' Grant muttered. 'See how that hide is roan. It's smaller than the last one too. Who selected the bulls?'

'Blessed Virgin, I should have thought of that,' said Maruffo. 'Sforza probably bribed the pageant director.'

The Florentine knight had ridden over to his servant and taken a crossbow. 'Exactly,' said Grant. 'They've given this man a bull that won't charge. Howsoever he kills it now, it will look shameful after the show Alessandro Sforza just put on.'

The crowd were not approving of the knight shooting the bull at a distance from the horse. He struck it three times, rewinding the bow in the saddle. It was commendable marksmanship, but it offended the crowd's sense of fairness.

Then the bow was exchanged for a half-moon blade on a long pole which the Florentine knight used to hamstring the animal from behind. Catcalls rained down from the benches as he dismounted and approached the bull with his sword to deliver a coup de grâce.

'He's been humiliated,' said Maruffo. 'I wonder what Sforza has arranged for you.'

Since Grant's turn was next, they did not wait long to find out.

When the red wooden door swung open and Grant's bull

trotted out, he felt his nerves stretch to their quivering limits. The beast was to bull as wolf to dog.

The specimen Sforza had fought had seemed large, but this one dwarfed it. Standing high on its legs, long in the body with huge shoulders, a cresting neck muscle and pair of wide horns, the monster eyed Grant across the arena, pricked its ears and without hesitation, charged.

It was a matter of pride to John Grant that no man should ever prove braver than him. Faced with such a beast, at little cost to his dignity, he might have skirted the ring like the previous knight. He might have called for a bow or even an arquebus. Instead he tried to emulate Alessandro Sforza.

But even Sforza would have been no match for this dreadful animal.

Grant kept his horse under the tightest of control, stepping, as he had seen Sforza do, in a tight circle to try and force the bull to fruitlessly expend all its explosive power.

He was almost successful.

This bull, more cunning than the other, hid its capacity and did not give a single chop of its horns, or bring its head too low, until it was sure of the range. Then, on the second turn, it struck with the precision of a dagger stroke.

The belly of Grant's horse rent open as if it were a purse of silk.

Maruffo leapt over the parapet before he knew what he was doing. He had seen the horse lift off the ground as the cruel, needle point horns struck. He had seen Grant thrown and trusted that the Scotsman would know how to fall and roll clear before his dying mount came thrashing down onto him.

Maruffo had no great knowledge of bulls, but he was sure

such a malevolent beast would look first to finish off its prey. It had the power in its hooves to break a human skull like cheap crockery. He needed to distract it for however long it took Grant to get clear.

'Huh! Huh! Huh!' Maruffo shouted, waving his arms as he ran a few steps towards the middle of the fighting pit. 'Hey, over here!'

In his ears he could hear the noise of the crowd, a great stew of screams and cries and cheers.

The bull was still intent on its first victim - the horse - and drove its head with a corpse-jarring butt against the thrashing hind quarters. Maruffo saw Grant skip away from the carnage. He seemed uninjured. Then the bull glanced up from the horse and turned its glare onto the new challenger in its territory. Maruffo stopped in his tracks, waved his arms one last time, and fled for the barrier.

He tumbled over the spread cape and sat on the ground with his back against the wood while he caught his breath. He grinned up at the long-bearded Greeks and the girls behind, and saw their eyes widen just as the wall at his back shook like an earthquake. He heard the snort of air from the bull's nostrils and the scrape of horns in the wood. He felt the thrum in the earth as its hooves came down and could still feel them, faintly, once it turned and made off.

When at last he mustered the courage to climb to his feet and look back over the parapet, Maruffo discovered that Grant had been thrown a lance by another of the knights and was facing the monstrous bull on foot.

'Holy Virgin protect him!' Maruffo implored. He wanted to cover his eyes as the stampeding bull rushed at the young Scotsman. The lad had come from the wars in France. Grant was tougher than any soldier Maruffo had fought with or against and he was too stupid to know when to cut and run.

Appropriately, Grant had set himself into the guard of the ox, with the lance held high by his head as if it were his own single horn. The bull closed in and with his swordsman's quick feet, Grant twisted away from the lowered horn and brought his lance tip down to meet the bull's neck.

The bull's momentum drove it onto the lance. The warhead sank deep in the crest of muscle and struck the bull's spine like a falling star meeting earth.

All Grant's weight and stubborn strength was set in his guard. The bull had all its natural power. The lance, caught between, bowed almost double and snapped, dislocating Grant's wrist; pieces of the broken shaft cartwheeled away across the dirt.

The bull continued its pass across the arena, the blood bubbling up from the wound and running slick down its sides like lava from a cinder cone. The beast did not bellow or show much discomfort, but for a time it kept to the far side of the arena and watched its opponent warily from under its lowered horns.

With his good hand, Grant picked up the pieces of the broken lance and carried them back to the barrier.

Maruffo offered him a replacement. 'Should your hand look like that?'

Grant took the new lance and shot a black look toward the bull. 'To hell with the hand.'

Turning, he strode back out to reclaim the middle of the ring. The bull took up the challenge. With a paw of the earth, it rushed at him once more. Grant placed the new lance into his right hand, reset his guard, and thrust.

Again he struck vertebrae. Again he drove on. Again the lance bowed. This time it did not snap because the ruined ligaments of his wrist gave out first.

Grant did not look to Maruffo for another lance. Instead, as the bull cantered to the barrier and turned, he retrieved the same one from where it had landed. Deliberately, he used his right hand, his teeth grinding together from the pain.

For a third time Grant set his feet and sighted the charging beast down the lance's shaft. The tossed horns passed close enough to unpick a cowrie shell from his doublet as he plunged the lance home. But the weapon again hit bone and flew into the air.

As Grant bent to take up the lance again, the crowd were begging him, 'No, no, no, no!' As if hearing them, the right hand refused to lift it. Smashing the disobedient limb furiously against his hip, Grant picked up the shaft with his good hand and stubbornly put it into his right.

The bull had gone back to relive its victory with the horse, nudging a questing horn at the still corpse. Stung three times, it would no longer charge. It simply stood and watched Grant approach.

At any time, without further discomfort or peril, Grant could have called for the crossbow or driven his lance at the beast's throat; but he did not even consider it.

However cynical his feelings that morning when Maruffo had described the contest as a matter of honour, it was certainly that now. His stubborn pride required that he slay his opponent with a lance between the shoulders, going in over the horns as Sforza had done, and to hell with the fact he was not mounted.

Finally, at the fourth time of asking, the metal tip found

the gap between skull and spine. Standing hollow-eyed and breathless, the sweat shining like pearls in his beard, Grant saw the bull sway and topple, lifeless, into the dust.

His swollen wrist had doubled in size, but when Grant pulled the lance out, he still used his right hand, to chastise its earlier refusal. Then, teeth bared, he shifted the shaft to his left and, without a glance to the crowd, walked back to the wooden parapet.

His eyes stared far into the distance. His battle rage had vanished, but its euphoric effects had not yet given over fully to the reality of his injury. When Maruffo asked once more about his hand, Grant looked at him blankly. He was not thinking about his hand at all. He was thinking about the bull.

Then at last he seemed to register Maruffo. The blunt stare honed itself to a knifepoint. 'Next time, kill the damned beast yourself.'

He did not wait for Maruffo's answer, nor to see the Milanese agent come smiling down off the benches. Instead, stamping out from the arena, Grant found the nearest tavern to drown his wrist pain in a wine pot, and the ladies of Florence suffered no risk to their honour from Scotland that carnival night.

Interview with Peter Sandham

Can you tell us a bit about yourself? How long have you been writing and what other jobs have you had?

I'm originally from the west of England but have been living in Hong Kong for the past six years. I have always loved history and studied politics and philosophy at university before stumbling into a career in finance. I have written stories since childhood but only began to take my writing seriously about twelve years ago. I had the turmoil of the Global Financial Crisis in my day job and my first child had just been born, so writing was a great outlet.

What is it about the Medieval Period that inspires you?

My own corner of the Medieval Period is its final decades. I like a knight and a castle as much as anyone, but what I love about those last years is the upheaval – technical, societal and marshal. They are the birth pangs of our modern world and I am in awe of the people who had to deal with those profound shifts. For example, the main character in my writing is a real historical figure, Anna Notaras. Anna was born in a Roman Emperor's court and yet lived to see the New World's discovery. She survived the Fall of Constantinople – which we might argue was history's first successful deployment of massed gunnery - and funded the first Greek printing press in Venice. She did all that despite the triple medieval disadvantage of being a woman, a refugee, and a religious minority. Another major figure from my books is Mara Brankovic who overcame similar hurdles to be an influential figure in the Ottoman court and a significant player in diplomatic relations between the warring Ottoman and Venetian empires. There is so much more to the medieval period than the stock characters people expect to encounter. I love uncovering real figures who overturn those stereotypes – the pope who wrote erotic novels and had two children out of wedlock; the Ottoman grand vizier who had a network of relatives from a range of religious faiths stretching around the levant; the feared Italian mercenary whose enemies only discovered was a woman when they peeled the armour from her corpse. Hollywood can't invent better.

What inspired you to write this particular story?

In the first book in my series, Porphyry and Ash, we meet a Scottish mercenary called John Grant. It was learning of the historical Grant that first sparked my interest in the period. I wanted to know what a lone Scotsman was doing on the far side of Europe winning plaudits at the Fall of Constantinople. It turns out his life prior to 1453 is a blank space, but in my novel there wasn't the chance to flesh out much of his earlier life. Equally, the Council of Florence in 1439 was a significant moment in the Byzantine empire's final years but again, too detached from the events of 1453 to be included in Porphyry and Ash. So I jumped at the chance to show Grant as a younger man still learning his trade and tying it in with the Council of Florence felt cool. The idea of destiny arises in the novel and I enjoyed creating in this short story a moment that is almost an unconscious tying of a thread between Grant's life and the culmination of his purpose. In that context the bull's death shown here becomes almost a sacrificial rite, binding the fate of Grant to the empire, even if he will not realise it (if at all) until many years later.

What do you enjoy most about writing?

I love plotting. I love connecting the disparate threads of lives and events and weaving a narrative that joins them together.

If you were transported back to the time your story is set, who is the first person you would want to talk to and why?

So hard to choose just one! I will say my antagonist, Mara Brankovic. She would have insights on everything from Ottoman, Byzantine and Venetian sides.

If there was one event in the period you could witness (in perfect safety) what would it be?

It would have to be the final days of the Siege of Constantinople. I'm not sure my heart could stand it though.

Why do you think readers are still so thirsty for stories from this period?

Well the period never seems to run out of unexplored corners to uncover. Things were so different, so it makes for great escapist tales and yet we all grow up with stories of kings and queens and acts of chivalry, so there is a reassuring familiarity to the world the reader is immersed in.

What are you writing at the moment?

The third novel in my series, Porphyry and Frankincense. It is set in Rome and Gothia, which was a tiny Byzantine enclave in the Crimea that managed to continue for another twenty-two years after the fall of Constantinople. The Rome section explores the murder plot in 1468 against Pope Paul II by an eccentric group of Neoplatonist scholars.

How important is it for you to be part of a community of writers, and why?

Moral support is always important, the more so from people in the same boat. Family and friends will give encouragement but perhaps less constructive criticism and technical advice. For that a community of writers can really help each other grow.

Where can readers find out more about your books?

I am on twitter: @HKSandham and I occasionally blog at porphyryand.blogspot.com

A Night Journey by Helena Schrader

Jerusalem
August 1187

John was terrified. He knew as the son of a baron of Jerusalem, he shouldn't be. He knew he *ought* to feel angry and defiant. He ought to want to fight for his faith, for Christ, for the Holy Sepulcher. He ought to believe that God would rescue them, that there would be a miracle. But he didn't.

Taking advantage of his mother's meeting with the Patriarch of Jerusalem and other dignitaries behind closed doors, he evaded his tutor to slip unnoticed into the street. He wanted to find out for himself what was *really* going on.

John knew the Syrian quarter around the family residence well. He'd been out in these streets many times before. The Ibelin palace stood at the busy intersection of the Street of the Spaniards and Jehoshaphat street. John's realm stretched from the Gate of St. Stephens to the Jehoshaphat Gate, including the whole northeast corner of the city.

Although it was normally only a short walk to St. Stephen's gate, today John had a hard time making his way against the stream of refugees flooding in. The sight of them filled John with resentment bordering on panic. There were so many of them, and every day — every hour — there were more. Yet, his mother rebuked him when he complained about them clogging the streets with their broken-down wagons, handcarts, and lame donkeys.

"We are refugees too," she'd reminded him. "But by the Grace of God we have a home to go to. These poor souls do not."

John hadn't dared talk back to his mother, but he feared if too many people came to Jerusalem, there wouldn't be enough food or water for them all. His mother had already turned over the entire back courtyard to refugees, and John and his siblings shared a bed to make room for their aunt and cousins. Even his mother, a dowager queen, shared her bed; she slept with her daughter by her first marriage, John's half-sister Isabella.

John didn't know how much food they had in the larder, but it *couldn't* be enough for all the people they were feeding. Not for long. Every single day they consumed mountains of bread, rounds of cheese, and barrels of wine. Nothing would last for long at that rate, and then what would they do? The Saracen army had chased the farmers from their fields and driven off the livestock. The gardens around Jerusalem were abandoned — or simply picked clean by the hordes of refugees. No more food was coming into the city, only extra mouths to feed.

Yet a water shortage would be even worse, John thought. It was high summer, and there was little hope of rain for weeks. What if the wells ran dry?

John looked up at the naked sky burning down on the dusty city, and his nose took in the smell of sweat, urine, feces, and dust that accompanied the refugees. They seemed to be poorer and dirtier every day. His mother said that was because, with each passing day, the refugees came from farther away. Anyone who lived nearby had sought shelter behind the city walls on the very first day or two.

Just yesterday, John had encountered refugees all the way from Acre. The bustling port city, with its massive walls and high towers, had surrendered without a fight. Instead, the Count of Edessa had negotiated a surrender that allowed the Christian residents forty days to remove themselves and all their portable valuables, but the citizens had rioted in protest. John heard one of the refugees complain that Edessa, the queen's fat and greedy uncle, had been more interested in rescuing his sizable fortune than defending the most important port in the Kingdom of Jerusalem. "Acre could have held out! We could have defended ourselves 'till doomsday! The Greeks or Sicilians would have brought reinforcements within weeks. Eventually, all of Christendom would have come to our aid. We could have held Acre! Edessa's just a greedy coward! All the barons are a bunch of idiots! We've been led by idiots ever since good King Baldwin, God rest his soul, died, and that bitch and her lover usurped the throne!"

The anger in the man's voice unsettled John because he wasn't the only one on the streets blaming "the barons" for the disaster. The "barons," they claimed, had led the Christian army to an unnecessary defeat. John didn't want to believe that because John's father was one of those barons. He had commanded the rearguard.

Yet John could not ignore what he was hearing either. One priest, who had been a knight before he lost his arm and turned to God, declaimed publicly: "You don't have to be a genius to know an army can't get far in high summer without water. Why did King Guy ever leave the Springs of Sephorie? It was madness!"

That had been yesterday. John wanted to hear what they were saying today.

At St. Stephen's gate, he found a cluster of shopkeepers surrounding a recently arrived turcopole. They were chattering excitedly in Arabic, a language John spoke as well as French. The turcopole, a lean man in his late fifties to judge by his lined face and white hair, was reporting, "...he turned back south to rejoin forces with his brother al-Adil after the surrender of Botron—"

"So, he didn't take Tripoli?" one of the shopkeepers asked hopefully. That sounded like the first good news in a month.

"No, he stopped short of Tripoli and turned back with his mounted troops, leaving the infantry to occupy Sidon, Beirut, Gibelet, and Botron."

"Has Beirut fallen?" another shopkeeper asked in alarm.

"Beirut resisted, and everyone inside was slaughtered or enslaved," the turcopole confirmed.

The others crossed themselves and muttered various expressions of shock or sadness, except for the man who'd asked the question. He gasped and cried out, "my mother, my poor mother! Enslaved at age 62! How is this possible?"

The others nodded in mute sympathy, but then someone asked, "Where's Saladin now?"

"He's joined his brother outside Ascalon."

"What about Jaffa?"

"Same fate as Beirut. The fierce resistance provoked al-Adil's wrath, and he allowed his soldiers a bloodbath when they finally broke in. Not many survived to be enslaved — women and children mostly, almost no one else."

"And now al-Adil and the Sultan are both besieging Ascalon?"

"Yes. They say the Sultan had King Guy with him and was going to use him to force the city to surrender."

"How? If he offered to torture Guy in front of the people of Ascalon, they would probably cheer him on!"

Several of the others hushed the outspoken man and looked over their shoulders hastily. King Guy might be in Saracen captivity, but his wife Queen Sibylla was right here in Jerusalem. Neither she nor the Patriarch would take kindly to disrespectful remarks like this. "Guy was to order it."

"And you think he will?"

The turcopole shrugged, "Who knows? I need to water my horse. We can talk later."

The little circle broke up, and John continued his wandering, too restless to return home. He stopped to watch the Norse armorer, glistening with sweat, as he hammered at an axe on his anvil. John was fascinated by the craft of making weapons from red-hot steel, but he was pushed aside by a customer coming in.

John found himself before the great convent of St. Anne. He joined the large crowd standing in the forecourt, listening to Mass being sung inside. The nuns' harmonious and melodic voices wafted out of the open doors, high, yet clear. John imagined this was the way angels sounded, but he didn't have the patience to stay and listen.

He sauntered over to the nearby bathhouse, only to find it so swamped with dirty humanity that he hastily moved on as far as the tall, intimidating wall surrounding the Temple precinct. On the other side of this wall was the headquarters of the Knights Templar. John would have liked to go in. He'd heard servants talking about how "gigantic" the hall was, and his mother had spoken of the beauty of the churches. The complex could house hundreds of knights and just as many sergeants and turcopoles.

Yet now it was almost empty. The Templars had ridden with the feudal army of Jerusalem to confront Saladin's most recent invasion. They had taken all their knights, sergeants, and turcopoles. The entire fighting strength of the Knights Templar had been wiped out at the battle fought at Hattin. Although there were rumors the Master had been taken prisoner by Saladin, not one Templar had returned to Jerusalem. That meant that on the other side of the great, white wall, only a handful of men — too sick, old or ill to fight — remained.

John stood, indecisively looking around. He didn't want to return home yet. He considered risking the walk to the Holy Sepulcher but was intimidated by the masses of people he'd find there. It would be worse than Easter, he told himself, while the vast Hospitaller complex next door would be swarming with exhausted, sick, and wounded refugees. There was hardly anyone at the Hospital to look after them, John reasoned, because the Hospitallers too had been at Hattin, and taken their field hospital staff with them. Left behind were the decrepit, the handicapped, and the sisters. The later might help the sick and injured, but they couldn't defend the walls of Jerusalem.

That was what terrified John.

Everywhere he looked he saw exhausted women, crying children, priests, monks, nuns, old men, and fat tradesmen, but no fighting men. The Norse armorer might be able to fight, John supposed, and Master Shoreham with the dozen sergeants he'd brought from Ibelin, but John hadn't seen a single *knight* since arriving in Jerusalem.

How could they defend Jerusalem without knights? With only a handful of sergeants and turcopoles?

One of the sisters at St. Anne's had told the crowd yesterday that "the saints" would fight for Jerusalem. A priest had promised "a heavenly host of angels" would come to their aid.

John just didn't believe them. He was more inclined to believe the gossip that ran along the gutters like the sewage of the overcrowded city; *they were going to fight in order to die a martyr's death.* The apprentices and day laborers, even the younger monks and priests, were promising themselves a ticket to heaven. The way they talked about it, almost bragging about the futility of their sacrifice, made John's blood run cold despite the oppressive heat of summer.

If the men died a martyr's death as the Patriarch had told his mother they would, what would happen to the women and children?

John knew the answer. It was the answer of Beirut and Jaffa: slavery.

The thought of slavery made John sick to his stomach. As a slave, he would be separated from his family — his mother, brother, and sisters. He could be beaten or starved and forced to do anything just for food, water, and to avoid being hurt. He would have to work from dawn to until late into the night. He would sleep on the bare floor, kicked around and insulted by anyone and everyone. He might be sent to the dye-works where the slaves worked in vats of urine, or be made to clean the latrines of public baths, or walk — like a donkey — around and around in endless circles turning a mill wheel. Or — according to one of the grooms — sometimes the Saracens "neutered" boys by cutting off their penises so they could guard the harems of the rich.

John thought he would rather die than suffer slavery, but how could he make sure they killed him? No one was going to give him a weapon. Maybe if he attacked the Saracens, he could provoke them into killing him?

Or maybe, just maybe, his father would come and rescue him.

His father was alive and free. He had been one of the few fighting men to escape the trap at Hattin. He had led a charge late in the day and broken through the surrounding Saracens. With what was left of the rearguard, he'd punched a hole in the Saracen lines large enough for several thousand soldiers to escape. They had made it to the Sea of Galilee, and from there to the Templar castle at Saphet. After two days' rest, John's father had led the survivors on to Tyre, the most defensible of all Christian cities. Here they had taken over the defenses and sent word to all of Christendom what had befallen the Kingdom of Jerusalem. The Kings of Sicily and Hungary, of France and England, of Aragon and Castile, the Holy Roman Emperor, and the Emperor of the Greeks — they would all take the cross and come East to rescue Jerusalem.

But John wasn't an idiot. He knew — well, *sensed* — how far away Constantinople, Palermo, and Paris were. They would never get here in time.

John's father, on the other hand, was only as far away as Tyre, with several thousand fighting men who had survived Hattin. His father could still rescue him — if he wanted to.....

The sky around John was darkening, and the air was becoming hot and oppressive. It was like the first Good

Friday when the Romans had crucified Jesus Christ *here,* in Jerusalem — just across St. Stephens Street behind the Syrian Exchange under the small, grey dome he could clearly see.

John froze in his tracks as the strange darkness blotted out the sun and took away the air he was trying to breathe. He was paralyzed by what he was experiencing. When Christ had died on the cross one thousand one hundred and fifty-four years ago, the sun had hidden her face in grief. Now, again, like a Muslim maiden, the sun pulled a black veil across her face.

Was this a second Good Friday? The thought was terrifying, and sent a shiver down John's spine.

But — but — maybe it was the prelude to salvation?

Out of nowhere, disembodied, his father spoke to him. "The Lord will aid you if it pleases Him. My duty is to the kingdom."

"Father!" John cried out in horror. "I might be killed or enslaved! Father!"

A second time his father answered: "The Lord will aid you if it pleases him."

John's terror — no, his sense of betrayal — was so great that he cried out again. "Father! No!"

The cry broke through his slumber and tore him out of his dream.

Jolted from his sleep, his limbs knocked the small table beside the bed, and it scraped against the wall. Then he lay still, staring at the white linen canopy over the bed, listening to his breathing.

Beside him, his second son, Sir Baldwin, half-woke and through squinting eyes asked. "Is something wrong, Father?"

"No. Go back to sleep."

Baldwin was soon snoring softly again, but John lay awake in the darkness of the unfamiliar chamber at the royal castle of St. Hilarion trying to understand his dream. It had been so vivid, more like a memory than a dream, until the ending. There had been no darkness at noon when he was in Jerusalem. More important, his father had not abandoned him to the grace of God. His father had humbled himself before his worst enemy and had crossed Saracen-held territory — unarmed and accompanied by only a single squire — *to rescue his son.*

It was not his father who had told his son: "The Lord will aid you if it pleases Him." The words were his own. He had used them in response to the desperate situation of his son Balian, his father's namesake.

Did it matter that Balian was a skilled knight rather than a child?

Balian's life had been at risk. He had been surrounded by enemies. At least a half-dozen Sicilian knights had hacked at him from all sides.

John's younger sons, his knights, *his king* had all begged him to go to Balian's assistance. Yet he had answered: "The Lord will aid him if it pleases Him."

John, the powerful Lord of Beirut, shuddered in the pre-dawn darkness. A profound sense of unease replaced the childish terror of his dream. It had indeed pleased the Lord to save his son, but what judgment would the Lord serve on the father?

And would either Balian, his father or his son, ever forgive him?

Interview with Helena Schrader

Can you tell us a bit about yourself? How long have you been writing and what other jobs have you had?

I've been writing stories since I was seven and completed my first novel while still an undergraduate. However, I made a conscious decision not to try to earn my living as a writer. I was afraid that I'd end up writing what the market wanted rather than listening to my inner voice. Instead, I worked in consultancy and as an investor relations manager for financial institutions until I joined the U.S. diplomatic corps. I served primarily as an Economic Officer in Europe and Africa, retiring in 2018 from my last post, Ethiopia.

What is it about the Medieval period that inspires you?

The singularly meaningless term 'Middle Ages' covers roughly a thousand years of history across a continent. I can't say I'm particularly interested in all of it. However, I became fascinated with the crusader states during a trip to Cyprus twenty years ago. The idea of Western Europeans settling in the Eastern Mediterranean and creating sophisticated, multi-cultural feudal kingdoms at the cross-roads of civilizations fascinated me. The more I read and learned, the more I realized that much of what we learn in school — at least with respect to the crusades and the Middle Ages generally — is, to be polite, an oversimplification. Medieval society was richer, more sophisticated and in many ways more democratic that we are usually led to believe — much less what you see in Hollywood films or read in poorly researched novels. I suppose, a sense of indignation about all that misinformation inspired me to write about the period in an effort to set the record straight in some small way.

What inspired you to write this particular story?

I must confess, short stories are not my media. I write both non-fiction and fiction, but my non-fiction works usually run about 100,000 words and my novels are often double that. On being invited to contribute to this anthology, however, I realized that the prologue to my next full-length novel would work as a stand-alone short story. At least I hope it does!

So, the question becomes: what inspired me to write my current series of novels?

The series covers, in fictional form, the civil war between Frederick II and his vassals in Outremer during the second quarter of the 13th century. The revolt against Frederick II is one of those historical events that begs for a novel — or ten. On the one hand, you have one of the most colourful of medieval monarchs, a man who called himself 'the wonder of the world' and to this day is considered by many a genius and a man of tolerance far ahead of his time. On the other hand, a cast of rebels who were scholars and intellectuals, poets and patrons of the arts, supported by the commune of Acre. Add to that the relevancy of the issues at stake: the rule of law versus autocratic power, the right of citizens to defend themselves against tyranny, the point at which justice should give way to forgiveness — and vice versa. And much more, of course, like a wonderful but historically documented love story.

What do you enjoy most about writing?

That's a hard question because I love almost every aspect of writing — from the research to the polishing and perfecting of a finished manuscript. I have said elsewhere that writing a scene for the first time is rather like eating Tiramasu — or whatever sweet you love best. It's as exciting and invigorating as a shot of caffein. I never really know where a scene is going to end when I start writing it for the first time because I let the inspiration flow through me. I set my brain aside as much as possible and attempt to get inside my characters, to see the world through their eyes, and simply describe what they are seeing, doing, thinking, and feeling. The goal in the first draft is to let the characters lead rather than to manipulate and control them. Once the first draft is finished, however, I enjoy stepping back outside the characters and crafting a better product with the objectivity of an outsider looking at the impact of all aspects of scene and the selection of words. I've compared that to eating fresh baked bread — maybe not as delightful as eating sweets, yet in many ways more satisfying.

If there was one event in the period you could witness (in perfect safety) what would it be?

I rather like the idea of watching the ordinary people of Acre expressing their feelings for Frederick II by pelting him with entrails, bowels and guts as he made his through the city to sail away. It was a wonderfully creative form of nonviolent protest. There are leaders today that I would enjoy seeing in the same predicament.

Why do you think readers are still so thirsty for stories from this period?

Do you think they are? I hope so. I'm honestly not sure, but if readers are keen to read about the Middle Ages then perhaps because tales of knights in shining armor still resonate with many of them?

What are you writing at the moment?

I'm working on two projects, one fiction and one non-fiction. The fiction project is a four-part series about the conflict between Emperor Frederick II and the people of Outremer led by John d'Ibelin in the early thirteenth century. Ibelin, often referred to as the "Old" Lord of Beirut, was the son of Balian d'Ibelin, who was featured in the (terribly inaccurate) Hollywood film *The Kingdom of Heaven*. The first two books in this series, released in 2018 and 2019 respectively, are: *Rebels against Tyranny* and *The Emperor Strikes Back*. The non-fiction project is the first of two books commissioned by Pen & Sword on the Latin East. *The Holy Land in the Era of the Crusades: Kingdoms at the Crossroads of Civilizations* brings together recent scholarly research on the crusader states and provides an overview in a single, readily accessible and affordable format. You can find out more about my books and awards at: http://helenapschrader.com or follow me on twitter at: @HelenaPSchrader.

Printed in Great Britain
by Amazon